Praise for Joshua Mohr's *SOME THINGS THAT M*

"Meet Rhonda, a man who spends his hau
Dumpster diving for redemption. With his ⎯ ⎯ ⎯ ⎯ ⎯ ⎯ ⎯ ⎯ ⎯ ⎯ ⎯ ⎯ ⎯ ⎯ ⎯ ⎯ ⎯ ιι like to
brag about the night I saved a hooker's life" – debut writer Joshua
Mohr sucks you into *Some Things That Meant the World to Me*. Charles
Bukowski fans will dig the grit in this seedy novel, a poetic rendering
of postmodern San Francisco."
—O, THE OPRAH MAGAZINE
#8 OF "10 TERRIFIC READS OF 2009"

A BEST BOOK OF 2009 "This trippy, hypnotic and volatile little novel packs
immense punch into a slim volume. Mohr's debut shows more than
promise for a rich, risk-taking future."
—THE NERVOUS BREAKDOWN

"Where Michel Gondry would go if he went down a few too many
miles of bad desert road. Replace the director's *Science of Sleep*-style
clouds-of-cotton whimsy with harsh whiskey and hot sand and you get
a sense for the dark world Mohr constructs."
—THE COLLAGIST

"Embrace[s] and affirm[s] the value of the lives we're in."
—THE SACRAMENTO BEE

"Mohr's prose roams with chimerical liquidity. The magic of this book
is a disturbing, hallucinogenic magic."
—BOSTON'S WEEKLY DIG

"Biting and heartbreaking, a piercing look at the indelible scars a violent
past has left on a young man named Rhonda. Mohr uses punchy,
tightly wound prose to pull readers into a nightmarish landscape, but
he never loses the heart of his story; it's as touching as it is shocking."
—PUBLISHERS WEEKLY (STARRED REVIEW)

"What Joshua Mohr is doing has more in common with Kafka, Lewis
Carroll, and Haruki Murakami, all great chroniclers of the fantastic.
He's interested in something weirder than mere sex, drugs, and
degradation."
—THE RUMPUS

TERMITE PARADE

a novel

JOSHUA MOHR

TWO DOLLAR RADIO
Books too loud to ignore.

TWO DOLLAR RADIO is a family-run outfit founded in 2005 with the mission to reaffirm the cultural and artistic spirit of the publishing industry.

We aim to do this by presenting bold works of literary merit, each book, individually and collectively, providing a sonic progression that we believe to be too loud to ignore.

Copyright © 2010 by Joshua Mohr
All rights reserved.

ISBN: 978-0-9820151-6-2
Library of Congress Control Number: 2010927793

Front cover art by Aubrey Rhodes.
Author photograph by Leota Antoinette Higgins.
Typeset in Garamond, the best font ever.

No portion of this book may be copied or reproduced, with the exception of quotes used in critical essays and reviews, without the written permission of the publisher.

This is a work of fiction. All names, characters, places, and incidents are products of the author's lively imagination. Any resemblance to real events or persons, living or dead, is entirely coincidental.

TWO DOLLAR RADIO
Books too loud to ignore.
www.TwoDollarRadio.com
twodollar@TwoDollarRadio.com

For those of us who want to do better.

CENTRAL ARKANSAS LIBRARY SYSTEM
LITTLE ROCK PUBLIC LIBRARY
100 ROCK STREET
LITTLE ROCK ARKANSAS 72201

TERMITE PARADE

Tûr•mīt – Any soft-bodied, social insects that live in colonies and are highly destructive.

PART I
WHAT WENT WRONG

MEET MIRED

There were days I felt like the bastard daughter of a *ménage a trois* between Fyodor Dostoevsky, Sylvia Plath, and Eeyore.

Days pungent with disappointment.

Days soiled and hoarding blame.

Allow me to offer some evidence: about 5 a.m. on the morning after my last birthday, I was on my knees in front of the toilet, leaning over it and looking down at the water, waiting to throw up again. I stared at my reflection and could see myself so clearly. My life in the toilet. I was right where I belonged.

MEET DEREK

I tried to make another whiskey on the rocks but there weren't any ice cubes left in the lousy freezer. Not that there's much of anything left except all my impossible, obscene questions: what's the difference between lying to yourself and being redeemed, what if they're identical, like me and my twin brother, Frank, what if they look exactly alike but are completely different monsters?

But here was one I could answer because while there weren't any ice cubes, there was a sack of frozen peas. So do I make a "whiskey on the peas"? Had I turned into that kind of person?

After the riot that had happened between Mired and me, the answer was easy, tearing open the bag and clutching a handful of green ice.

MIRED TELLS THE FIRST BIT OF THE ROMP

"There's nothing to worry about, Mired," the dentist said to me.

"I'm sure there's not," I said, or at least I did my best to say: I spoke with a lisp since knocking out my front teeth. Since I'd felt the maelstrom of humiliation, ruining not only my mouth, but breaking my wrist, stitches on my forehead, bruises all over my face, aching muscles in my back. "But I'd rather not remember anything. That's all."

"You'll be fine," he said, a tall man, with tall man's hands, not thick but stretched and lean, the kind with sparkling manicures you see in magazine ads. "Novocain will be enough." He smiled.

"I'd be more comfortable knocked out."

"We don't do that anymore. Not for this procedure."

"Can you make an exception?"

"No, but I can promise to be careful and gentle." He smiled again.

I didn't believe him. His words sounded too savvy, too adept coming from his mouth. He'd said them to a hundred skittish women. And, like me, those hundred skittish women knew he was lying but agreed anyway, because that was what we did: we swallowed every lie every man everywhere heaved in our ears.

———

For four hours my mouth was pried open. A pollution drifting out of it as the dentist drilled my broken teeth to thin posts.

These posts would anchor the temporary dental bridge. The dental bridge would be three shiny white teeth, so shiny and white that no one would be able to tell they were fake, he'd promised me. But before the shiny and white fake ones could be mounted in my mouth, the dentist had to do this: had to whittle my teeth into thin mounting posts.

The smell of hot, burning teeth was like microwaved tinfoil, but worse because I was the microwaved tinfoil. Worse still because this whole thing was my fault; I'd microwaved myself, getting drunk and acting like an imbecile and falling down the stairs. A grown woman falling down the stairs.

Every now and again, the drill shot a shard of tooth from my mouth, a few hitting me in the face, or landing on my bib, or flying onto the carpet.

"Would you like to rinse?" the dentist said.

I nodded. I took a sip of water and sloshed it around, some spilling from my numb lips. When I spat into the sink, slivers of my gums lodged in the drain and looked like the shavings from a pencil's eraser. Seeing my own gums clot there made it feel like everything was falling to pieces, like life was infinitely more complicated today from yesterday from the day before, and it didn't seem as though there was any chance things would ever be simple again, ever new, ever thrilling. It seemed as though the sheen of everything tarnished with time. Even my own sheen, as I dribbled dignity from my mouth in a river of drool and blood, slipping down the drain with my gum-shavings.

I wasn't aware that I shook my head until the dentist said, "Are you okay?"

"Can I go to the bathroom?"

"Of course."

I walked down the hallway, tried to open the bathroom door, but it was locked. Only had to stand there for a few seconds before Derek came out.

"This is horrid," I said.

"Is there anything I can do?"

"It hurts."

"Ask him to numb you more."

"I deserve it."

"What?"

I hugged him. I hugged him because I needed him to know that I was sorry, that I knew I was wrong and hoped he'd give me the chance to make things up to him. I needed him to know that I finally accepted my role in our problems. For months, I'd privately blamed every one of our swollen woes on Derek, his drinking, his ambivalence, his temper and wandering eye. But I couldn't continue to propel blame on him, not after making a lovely fool out of myself at Shawna's house, in front of all those people, and tumbling down our stairs.

"I hope you can forgive me," I said to Derek.

"There's nothing to forgive."

"We can get through this."

"Let's talk about it later."

"I love you."

"I love you, too," he said and walked back to the waiting room.

I went into the bathroom and shut the door. I still wore the dental bib, which had wild red splatters all over the front of it. With my fingers, I pushed my upper lip up. One of my teeth had been shaped into a thin post. I touched it and didn't feel a thing. I pushed my tongue against it. Nothing felt real. I put my hands over my face. *I'd done this to myself. Got jealous and lost control. No one to blame but me.*

What did Derek mean when he said, "Let's talk about *it* later"? What was "it"? Since when did he want to talk about anything?

Bleary eyed, I staggered back to the dental chair.

"All better?" the dentist said.

"Better than what?" I lisped, drooling from the Novocain.

———

After it was all over, I walked into the waiting room and Derek wasn't there. I said to the receptionist, "Did my boyfriend run an errand?"

Her eyes were light brown, almost amber, and like amber, they looked old, lifeless, cemented. "I don't know," she said and asked me how I'd like to pay.

I handed her a credit card and hoped it worked. "When did he leave?"

"A couple hours ago."

"Hours?"

She swiped my card. It was taking a long time to process.

"Did he say anything to you before he left?" I said. *Did he happen to tell you what he wanted to talk with me about later?*

Her amber eyes were fixed on the credit card machine. I was convinced that she was about to tell me my card was declined, and assumed that Derek wanting to talk later meant he'd soon be telling me our life was declined. Everything, everyone had reached their limits with me.

But it must have gone through, because she handed me the receipt and a pen.

At least I hadn't broken the wrist I wrote with. "Are you sure he didn't say anything?"

She looked at my fake teeth, then my eyes, then my fake teeth. "No, he simply walked out the door."

She made it sound like the easiest action in the world, walking out on me.

DEREK CATCHES US UP

ON WHAT REALLY HAPPENED...

I was just getting home from another lousy day at work, lousy month at work, getting home to my girlfriend who was an eight on the lousy-scale herself. The whole apartment stunk like burning brakes so I asked, "What's that smell?" while waving my hand in front of my nose, and Mired said, "Don't worry, dinner's almost ready." She said, "I had a great day, thanks for checking." She said, "Things need to change, Derek. They really do."

Let's up her status to a nine on the lousy-scale.

I thought Mired had murdered another of her dad's Filipino recipes, but she kept calling this dish "chicken parmesan." Problem was I'd seen plenty of chicken parmesan in my day, so I knew that the chicken wasn't supposed to be pounded flat as a tortilla or cooked so long that it took nine back-and-forths with a knife to get through the skinny bastard, and between you and me, I've never known chicken to smell like burning brakes. Mired must have noticed me scowling at the food because she said, "You can cook dinner anytime you want."

"It doesn't taste *that* bad."

"Such a ladies' man," she said.

Better bump her up to a 9.5.

After we chewed our burned-brakes chicken, we were off to a *Bon Voyage!* party for our friend, Shawna, who was moving to Cleveland to take a new job. It might not be totally true to say that Shawna was *our* friend. Shawna was my friend. We'd worked together, years ago, at an auto parts store and had dated for a few months. Mired was a jealous person in the first place, and she was of the opinion that Shawna still had a crush on me, though I kept trying to tell her that there was nothing going on between us.

The mood Mired was in during our burned-brakes dinner was enough for me to know she didn't want to say *Bon Voyage!* to anyone, let alone a woman she thought had a thing for me. She'd rather white knuckle through the party than sit home and wonder what styles of no-good me and Shawna were test-driving.

We arrived at the *Bon Voyage!*, and immediately Mired started drinking vodka tonics. Really drinking. Rock star drinking. Her piss-poor mood had gotten pisser and poorer right when we walked in because Shawna pronounced Mired's name wrong, calling her Meer-red.

"It's pronounced like the verb," Mired said to her. "You know: mired in depression, mired in immense mental anguish, mired in a diabolical vortex of low self-esteem."

"Got it," Shawna said.

"That's what you said last time," Mired said, batting her eyes like a sly homecoming queen.

While the other twenty guests and I were in the living room, talking about Shawna, and Cleveland, and all the opportunities that awaited her there, Mired sat alone in the kitchen, though we could all see her down the hallway from where we'd planted. Every once in a while she'd yell, "I'm sure going to miss you, Shawna," and she'd laugh real hard and these twenty other guests with their forty wide eyes just stared at her, pretending to be deaf, and I'd deflect by droning on about Cleveland being the best city splattered on our continent.

You see, all these surprised eyes weren't just learning that Mired drank too much and had a sailor's mouth and didn't like Shawna. No, they soaked up the fact that there was barely trust between Mired and me, and the trust we did have was heavy and rundown, a burden we lugged behind us like concrete shadows.

After an hour or so, and probably seven drinks, Mired blurted, "Derek, maybe as a going away gift you should have sex with Shawna."

Forty humungous eyes and twenty tongue-tied guests. Shawna looked at me. I was supposed to do something, this was clearly supposed to be handled by me, but I didn't know what to say, so I tried to change the subject, asking, "Does anyone know the average rainfall in Cleveland?" but no one was listening, all looking toward the kitchen at Mired. Shawna had this seething look on her face and she said, "Do you have something to say to me?" and Mired said, "Why do you ask?" and Shawna said, "Are you insulting me in my own house?" and Mired said, "Absolutely not," and Shawna said, "Because you can leave right now," and Mired said, "I'll be over here minding my manners," and we all went back to talking, Shawna throwing an occasional stink-eye at Mired.

Guests reluctantly nibbled on chips and slurped the bottoms of their empty cocktails, chewing ice cubes, everyone too uneasy to replenish supplies because that meant a trip into the kitchen, near Mired's mean mouth. I knew her well enough to assume that things would diffuse if the other stunned guests and I ignored her outbursts, and it worked for a while.

But then Mired slurred, "Shawna, are you sure you wouldn't like to give Derek a blowjob for old time's sake?"

Twenty other guests and forty scathing eyes, their naked disgust, all staring at Mired as she embarrassed herself, embarrassed us, me. Guilty by association. Their awed eyes ricocheted from Mired to Shawna to me and back around, a vicious carousel, all these gazes grazing each of us. There was no way I could talk Mired down from the heights of her lousiest conspiracy, the lousiest one of all because this time there were all these eyewitnesses, instead of just the two of us, berating each other.

"We'll all watch," Mired said, aiming another homecoming smile toward Shawna. "Make a big batch of popcorn."

"Out!" Shawna said, "out, out, out of my house!" and she hopped up and ran toward the kitchen, but some of the guests got in her way. Shawna turned to me and said, "Get her out of here," and I said, "Fine, fine," and Mired said to her, "Who do you think you are?" and I didn't even get a chance to say *Bon Voyage!* Instead, I helped Mired stagger to the door and stagger down the stairs, almost falling twice, and I put her in the passenger seat and drove us home, punching our address into my GPS and paying sharp attention to the speed limit because of the whiskey I'd had.

The whole ride she kept saying, "Drop me off and go give it to her."

"Shut up."

"At least let her jerk you off."

"Shut up."

"You treat me like a dog."

This was so god damn frustrating because there wasn't anything going on between Shawna and me, and I was tired of walking on eggshells. I didn't need to. Shouldn't eggshell-walking be reserved for people who were actually trying to hide something? I mean, all I wanted to do was go say *Bon Voyage!* to an old friend and now I had to listen to all this.

Our conversation vanished as Mired passed out right in the middle of our latest screaming match. I sat at a red light and thought about her earplugs. Mired wore them to sleep. She was the lightest sleeper I'd ever met. Even the refrigerator's compressor clicking on could wake her up. I remember thinking to myself right then that I wished I'd had my own pair of earplugs while we were at Shawna's: I could have sat there and I'd have had no idea what Mired was saying. I was thinking about how beautiful it would be to block out all those ugly words, and the light turned green but I stayed right there, couldn't bring myself to drive home yet. The light turned red again, which made me happy and I sat there feeling happy, but with an idling dread because I knew the light would eventually change, and this time there was a car behind me. I didn't want to get home, or wake her up, not without my own pair of earplugs.

I pulled up to our lousy apartment building, and Mired was out cold. I shook her, said, "Get up," but she didn't move or say anything. The key was still in the ignition so I turned the car on and found a radio station playing Lynyrd Skynyrd because Mired hated that hillbilly shit. I made the music blare and gave her a few shakes, but she didn't move so I shut the car off and went to her side, opened her door and said, "Let's go." She finally answered me by saying, "I can't," and I said, "Can you walk on your own?" but since her eyes had shut again and her head swiveled every direction like a broken compass, I knew she couldn't. I threw her arm around my shoulder and guided her. We only took two steps before her legs went boneless, flaccid, falling, but I was able to catch her, swooping her up in my arms, the way a groom carries a bride on their wedding night. We lived on the second story, and I started struggling up the stairs, and she said, "Admit you want to have sex with her," and I didn't say anything, didn't need to renovate her accusations. Concentrating on climbing those steps. If we were going to keep fighting, I didn't want to say anything until we'd barricaded ourselves in our apartment. So I tried to ignore her, tried pretending that I wore earplugs or that my ears were locked like safes and her words didn't know the combinations, but it didn't work. I had no guard from anything that came out of her mouth. Mired said, "Go back and screw her," and I tried to cinch my ears closed. I said, "Shut up," and she said, "I can't believe the way you treat me," and I said, "That makes two of us," and she said, "I deserve more than you," and I couldn't believe what I was hearing, couldn't fathom how she figured she deserved more. It didn't make any sense, since I was the one trying to do the right thing, trying to help my drunken girlfriend get up the stairs while she berated me for something that wasn't even true.

I was halfway there, only six steps left. My arms shaking. I looked at Mired's face as she kept telling me how much better she deserved, which got me thinking about how much better I deserved, which got me thinking that maybe everyone thought they deserved more, which led me to the very notion of love, and I remembered that old cliché: *If you love something set it free.* I knew that wasn't the end of it, that more words followed, but I couldn't remember what they were, and, frankly, I didn't care. All I wanted was to set her free and never hear her say another syllable. I arched my back because she seemed to be getting heavier with every step – she'd been getting heavier for months now, every time she forced me to appointments with our lousy couple's counselor, every time she said mechanics don't make enough money, every time we had our maintenance sex, something we did these days to avoid a breakdown, like getting an oil change. Heavier with all her suspicious fits about women she assumed I wanted to sleep with, because it wasn't always like this. She wasn't always like this. There were months, good months when we first got together, months when we never fought, going out to bars and shooting pool and laughing. Or we'd order pork fried rice and get stoned and stuff our faces till we couldn't eat another bite and we'd stroke each other's stretched bellies as we lay in bed, talking about our due dates, Lamaze classes, what colors we'd paint our babies' bedrooms.

Mired had the sexiest laugh, too. I'd told her so on our first date, and she said, "You're only saying that so I'll sleep with you tonight," and I said, "I'll say anything if you sleep with me tonight," and she, laughing again, said, "At least you're honest."

I stared in her eyes, I remember staring so ferociously into them. "For better or worse," I said, "I'll always be honest with you."

Now I craned our combined weight up to the next step, my biceps burning, arms unable to hold her as high, which put increased pressure on the small of my back. Mired said, "You should love me more, Derek, but you can't stop treating me like I'm a worthless dog," and I felt a puncturing, like a nail jammed into a tire, except there was no tire, just me. Like something had ripped into my skin and there I was, leaking affection and patience and resilience. Spilling love.

Before I really realized what I was doing, my feet worked their way around, doing a one-eighty on that thin step, and I faced the bottom, and Mired mumbled something but all I could make out was *worthless dog* and knew she'd said it again, so I let my arms go limp and dropped her and watched her hit right at my feet and flip backward and then bounce all the way to the bottom of the stairs and land in a contorted heap, tangled like human laundry.

She didn't make any noise, didn't move. Just lay there.

I didn't move or make any noise, either, standing and looking down at her. Horrified. Like I'd just slit my wrists and waited for my blood to drain. Not dead, but dying. Life over. Because I'd go to jail for years. Because you couldn't do something like this without monster consequences.

I looked around to see if anyone was watching. There didn't seem to be so I rushed down the stairs and crouched next to her mangled face.

I said, "Are you all right?"

I said, "Jesus, baby, you fell down the stairs!"

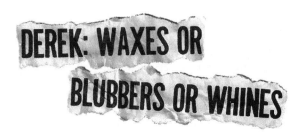

DEREK: WAXES OR BLUBBERS OR WHINES

I got Mired into our apartment and on the couch. Her front teeth were snapped to millimeters of jagged chalk. A gash on her forehead. An eye swelling closed. A lot of skin scraped from her face. She was still passed out, though moaning every once in a while and holding her wrist.

I called my twin brother and could only get out one syllable: "Shit."

"What?" Frank said, obviously asleep and surprised to hear from me.

"Come over," I said. "It's bad."

I guess given the way things turned out maybe I shouldn't have called him, but there was no way for me to know what was coming. See, I thought the riot had already happened – Mired rolling down the stairs – but that was only the beginning of our unrest, our uproar. The real riot hadn't detonated yet.

Or maybe things turned out exactly how they were supposed to. I don't know. I'm not the sort of guy who waxes philosophical or blubbers or whines about the way his life ends up. Point is I called Frank. Point is calling Frank changed everything.

MIRED: NONE THE WISER

I walked out front of the dentist's office to wait for Derek. It was mid-afternoon. The fog had come in. Windy. My hair blew in my face. I hugged myself, should have worn a wool coat, something heavier. The office was only a block off Union Square. Trolleys rang their bells as they went up and down the tracks on Powell Street. Tourists and shoppers combed from department stores to boutique outlets to overpriced restaurants, swinging their shopping bags with pride, cameras dangling and bouncing around their necks, San Francisco guidebooks in their adventurous hands, recommending that they go to Fisherman's Wharf and eat clam chowder out of sourdough bread bowls – and just why exactly was San Francisco famous for *New England* clam chowder? I wanted to scream at all of them. I loathed this part of town. It bothered me every time I heard a European or Asian language spoken: it meant that these people were away from their lives, had been granted pardons from their status quos. The only stamp on my passport in over ten years was a drunken weekend with Derek in Puerto Vallarta and really it was just like home – we drank and screwed and fought and drank and made up and screwed and that was our life.

I wiped my hand across my chin to see if there was any drool. There was. I called Derek's cell. He didn't answer. I left a message, slurring my words because of my numb mouth: *Hey, where are you? I'm finished. It really hurt. I want to go home and sleep so call me as soon as you pick this up.*

I opened the dentist's office door and sat down in the waiting room. No one else was there. The receptionist looked over at me.

"I'm waiting for my boyfriend," I said.

She nodded and pounded an index finger on her computer's keyboard.

I called Derek again and tried to whisper so the receptionist couldn't eavesdrop: *If I don't hear from you in the next five minutes, I'm taking a cab.*

I wanted to apologize again, wanted him to know that I was truly sorry for what had happened at Shawna's. I knew Derek; he didn't want to talk about things. So what else could I think when he said he wanted to talk later, except that he wanted to end our relationship? Derek, even Derek, had grown weary of me.

I fiddled with my cell phone. I was nervous, mad, woozy. I wanted to talk to someone. I called Veronica. No answer. I called Erin. No answer. I didn't leave messages.

I certainly couldn't call my mom. I didn't need any of her help hating myself right now and she wouldn't be able to resist the divine bait of commenting upon how stupidly I'd acted. How stupidly I always acted. Why, for reasons beyond her understanding, I was appalled at the very idea of seeking out and living a happy life. It was one of our last remaining topics of conversation, in our shrinking stable, the way I seemed to flourish in matters that disappointed her.

"My only daughter," she'd say, shaking her head as she endured the details of this or that from my life that were too absurd to be real.

"My only child," she'd lament, dying inside with the knowledge that I was her lone legacy, me and my unparalleled quest to make a million mistakes without learning a single lesson.

My mom never elaborated on these statements – *my only daughter, my only child* – but left their persecuting stink hanging between us. And as I sat in the waiting room, I didn't need any reminder of my life's fetid odor: it was all I could smell.

I decided to call Derek's brother, Frank. I hoped that he would think it shameful that Derek wasn't stationed in the waiting room, ready to take care of me. I needed someone to tell me that they found his absence as unforgivable as I did.

He picked up after two rings and said, "How's the mouth?"

"I've been better."

"What's wrong?"

"I'm at the dentist, and I don't know where Derek is."

"What?"

"He was supposed to wait for me. I just finished, and he's not here."

"Jesus Christ. I'll come get you," Frank said.

MEET FRANK THE FILMMAKER

Maybe it's the only reason people tell stories anymore: to clear their names.

That's what I tend to think, and that reasoning is my sole motive for talking to you in the first place, for getting involved in this ludicrous "deposition" – Derek's and Mired's bizarre, sadistic tale – this testimony of animals. I'll play the role of Reliable Eyewitness.

It was a Monday night when he summoned me to their apartment. It was the very next Friday afternoon when she called me for a ride from the dentist's. And it was later that Friday night/ early Saturday morning when all hell broke loose.

———

A couple quick things you have to know about me before you'll take this Reliable Eyewitness at his word. I am Derek's twin (or he is mine). I am an aspiring filmmaker. I am the mastermind behind *The Unveiled Animal*, which will soon be a brand name synonymous with cinema. Especially, now, that my true masterpiece is complete… but more on that to come.

Right before Mired called me from the dentist's, I'd just been treacherously reprimanded by my boss, but like any refined auteur, there's no reason for me to keep you at an arm's length from the action: go ahead and sneak closer, observe me in the wild, in the lush jungle of scene…

"Have you watched the Oscars, Frank?" my boss, Flo, said to me.

"I don't watch that tripe."

"But have you ever seen the show before?"

"It's been years…"

"Are you aware there is an awards program called the Oscars? That's what I'm asking you, Frank. Stop arguing with me. You are already on the very top of my shit-list. Just answer."

We were in her corner office. We'd just shown the new company training videos to the creative director, and he was "upset with our execution" and wondered if we had any "understanding of the agency's brand identity." He yelled at Flo in front of the production team; he directly criticized the editing, which was my responsibility.

Now Flo was directly criticizing me.

And I was pretending to care. This job peeled brain cells from me one by one, an occupational lobotomy, and I had to get out, had to save myself.

"Yes, I know the Oscars," I said.

"That's all I want you to say for a while. I'd like you to just sit there and shut up and listen. Oh, you can nod, if you need to express yourself. But as far as I'm concerned, you've expressed yourself enough for the time being. You expressing yourself is our current topic of conversation. And you may not have a job by the time this conversation is over. You need to know that's a possibility. You may get fired right now. That's how tired of your bullshit I am. So you just sit there and shut up and let me do some expressing for a change."

She looked at me and waited. I nodded. Biding my time. There was no reason to try and argue. She'd never understand. It wasn't possible to explain integrity to a charlatan. All she understood were bank statements and bottom lines and art was simply another commodity.

"That's exactly fucking right," she said. "Good. The Oscars. I asked you about the Oscars because I love watching that show. The pageantry. The celebrities and the beautiful gowns and the artistic competitions. My husband and I have a neighbor who hosts an Oscar party every year, and we go over there and watch the whole show, from beginning to end. I only pee during the commercial breaks so I don't miss a second of the excitement. That's how much I love the Oscars. Understand?"

I nodded.

Flo sat proudly behind her glass desk. I was in one of her uncomfortable armchairs. She was black, about sixty, and dyed her hair wine red and was famous around the agency for her meticulous designer outfits. One of the production assistants always counted the days between Flo wearing the same pair of shoes twice to the agency. Her record was sixty-seven straight.

"And because I never miss a second of the Oscars," she said, "I know with absolute certainty, that there's no category called 'Best Internal Corporate Training Video.' I know that there's never been a category called that and there never will be one called that. I know because internal corporate training videos are not art. They are marketing tools. They are resources that agencies use for many purposes, Frank, but none of those purposes are god damn art films."

She stopped and glared at me. I nodded again.

"We don't need god damn art films in corporate fucking training videos, and I don't need you making me look like I can't run my department, and I don't need my boss screaming in my fucking face because you're confused about your job responsibilities. You are here to edit training videos that map exactly to the company template. If you are bored or feel this assignment is beneath your gargantuan talents, then quit. Do you understand?"

I didn't nod. I needed a nudging from the nest. Before I ended up like her: jaded and complacent and dazzled by status. Seduced by a chain-gang wearing Dolce & Gabbana prison garb.

"You've been with us a long time," she said, "and I don't get why you're suddenly acting like a misunderstood artist. Aren't you a little old for this shit? It's time to act like a big boy. I know you can do your job because you've done it for years. Years! So what suddenly changed? Why are you suddenly too good to accomplish the elementary tasks that fall under your control? I don't understand. I thought you were happy here. I know this isn't your dream job. Hell, I'd be worried if it was. But we all have to pay the bills, Frank. This is a good living. You make a lot of money for doing bullshit. There's no reason to throw this all away. So what's it going to be? Can you drop the jilted art school shtick and act like a grownup, or do I need to find a replacement?"

I didn't nod or say anything.

Just one nudge from the nest and I'd be free.

"This is the part where you participate in the fucking conversation," she said.

I didn't nod or say anything and had a look in my eyes that begged *please, just one nudge, just one, please, and I'll have no choice but to remember who I am. An auteur.*

"This is serious, Frank, are you hearing me?"

I didn't nod or say anything.

"Do you want me to fire you? Do you want to get fired?"

I finally nodded. Each flight of the chin, yes yes yes, nudge nudge nudge.

"Why are you doing this?" she asked.

I stopped nodding. "I want to make real movies. I have to. I have to try before it's too late."

I really did. And I owed it all to Derek, dropping Mired down the stairs and inviting me into the aftermath. He'd reawakened my glorious thesis that there was indeed an *Unveiled Animal*. It was alive and vicious, and it was out there – it was in every one of us – and I could lure its savageness into my film, once I was free from Flo's bullying.

"Clean out your desk and give my regards to Steven Spielberg," she said. "I hear he's a big fan of yours."

THE TWINS TALK FAMILY LORE

Our old man was one of those Vietnam vets who barely acknowledged his kids because of what he'd done. Our phantom father. He'd been on a two-day pass in Saigon, two days to drink beers and screw whores and pretend that he hadn't been firing bullets at every sound a jungle made and hitting who knew what. Two days to blow off steam before his platoon made their way to My Lai. Yeah, that My Lai. He was only eighteen then, and he and his two army buddies came across an old local drunk who told them of a bar where they could pay to eat a cobra's beating heart right after the snake was gutted. So they went and waited their turn and paid the price and stood in front of a guy with a huge knife who reached into a bin and pulled out a live cobra and slit its bottom from the base of its head almost to its tail and he splayed its filleted body exposing its innards and reached inside the snake and grabbed the heart and used the knife to saw it free from its connections and he held the beating heart in the palm of his hand. Our old man and his two buddies stood there in awe smiling and excited and our old man volunteered to be the first one to eat it and the man placed it in his palm and our old man said he was surprised how warm it was and he watched the heart beat and beat and he said it felt like he was holding a tiny animal like holding a new kind of life and he kept watching it beat and beat and his buddies said come on already eat the damn thing and he popped it in his mouth but didn't chew it just taking a swig of beer and washing it down into his stomach.

DEREK

As soon as Frank walked in and saw her condition, he started in with his whole WE-NEED-TO-GO-TO-THE-HOSPITAL-RIGHT-THIS-VERY-SECOND! routine.

We were standing there, looking at her.

"She's really hurt," my brother said. He'd put on a few pounds since the last time I'd seen him. He was really pale, more than we usually were. We hadn't hung out much since getting evicted from our first San Francisco apartment. Frank and I had split from the same egg, and we'd been splitting farther ever since.

"She's fine. Except for her hand. I'm pretty sure it's broken."

"Derek, we have to go."

"It's just some bruises. Some dental work. No big deal."

"It's a big deal."

"We can't," I said and shouldn't have been drinking anymore. I knew that, not after all I'd already swallowed at Shawna's party. But a whiskey seemed like it might help my pulse slow down to double digits so I could make a smart decision. I motioned toward the kitchen and Frank followed me, then I poured a whiskey and stared at him.

"What happened to Mired?" he said.

"We went to a party. She drank too much. When we walked up our front stairs, she tripped and fell." I sat down at the table.

He stayed standing. "We have to get her some help."

"She'll be fine," I said and slammed my whiskey.

"Let's call an ambulance."

"Too expensive."

"I'm taking her to the hospital."

"We don't have any insurance."

"So what? Her hand is broken. Her teeth."

"Frank, I don't have a hoity-toity internet job like you."

"I work in marketing."

He'd gone all fancy on me a few years back. Swanky job and college degree and leased a souped-up Lexus that he considered a sports car and I considered ridiculous. His life had the whole ooh-la-la options package.

"You know what I'm trying to say," I said. "I can't afford it."

"I can pay."

"No chance."

"This isn't about you, Derek. This is about Mired."

He was wrong there. This was about both of us. We were tangled in this lousy knot together. I needed to know exactly what she remembered so I could stop worrying about going to prison. Then I could worry about her. I wanted to worry about her. I really did. Listen, I'm not saying she made me do it. Of course not. I'm only saying that I'm an average guy who'd had a couple cocktails and carried someone up the stairs, someone who kept saying terrible things and would not shut up and that person's words pulverized me and all I was doing was trying to help her and finally I said to myself, you know what, I don't think I want to help her if she's going to talk to me like this.

I got up from the table and poured another whiskey. I asked if he wanted one, and all Frank said was, "At a time like this," and I couldn't tell if that meant he wanted one or not so I made him a drink to be on the safe side. I handed him his and we let our glasses touch, though neither of us offered up any inspired words. I took a big sip. Frank set his down.

"I thought you called me to help," he said.

"I did."

"But we're just sitting here."

Then we heard Mired moan and say something that sounded like "eh-wic." I assumed it was my name. My brother and I ran in and kneeled down by the couch.

"Do you remember what happened?" I said to her.

Frank shot me a shocked face and said, "Mired, would you like to go to the emergency room?"

She didn't answer either of us. We waited about ten seconds. I held my breath for each of those lousy seconds but nothing came.

"What if she's bleeding internally?" Frank said.

"You watch too much TV."

A moan. From Mired. Quiet. Uncomfortable. "Why did you, eh-wic?" she lisped and slurred, the consonants totaled coming out of her mangled mouth. Her eyes were closed. It was like she wasn't even talking to me. Like the voice wasn't connected to a body. Floating through the air. A radio wave. "Why did you draaawwwww…?"

I looked at my brother and shrugged my shoulders and tried to look confused.

But Frank's eyes were furious. "Did you drop her?"

"She was passed out. I was carrying her. She wiggled out of my arms."

"Bullshit!" he said. "I'm taking her to the hospital."

"You can't."

"I am."

"I won't let you."

I blocked my brother's way. I blocked it because I couldn't let him take Mired to the hospital so she could make me the only bad guy, the rogue soldier in a situation where we'd both been wrong. Blocked it because I felt dumb for calling Frank in the first place. I was hoping for loyalty but all he offered was grief and opposition and his lousy logic.

I said, "Stop right there," and Frank said, "She needs help," and I said, "We'll get her help soon," and I put my hand out to halt him, but he pushed me, right in the stomach with both his fists, slamming me into the coffee table and knocking the wind out of me and I fell to the floor. I tried to grab his pants leg as he passed me by but couldn't breathe or move and I heard him say, "Mired, we're going now," and she said, "eh-wic?" and he said, "Shhh."

I tried to stand up, I really tried. I made every effort to get up off the floor as I heard Frank move toward the door, open and close it, then carry Mired down the stairs.

MIRED

I'd never been so pleased that Frank and Derek looked alike as when Frank walked into the dentist's office and the receptionist stared at him. She thought it was Derek. I could tell. She thought he'd gone home and changed his clothes. It never dawned on her that this might not be him, and I wobbled off the couch and hugged him, smiling at her over his shoulder. He had some chub on him but was nice and tall like his brother. Frank's black hair was a little longer than Derek's, who kept his a crew cut which he buzzed himself every couple weeks in our bathroom.

I closed my eyes and leaned my head on Frank's chest, a gesture that very well could have shocked him; he and I weren't usually affectionate with each other. But the receptionist didn't know that. All she saw was that my boyfriend had returned, and that he loved me very much, so stop thinking he was neglectful and cold and uncaring, because he was right here to take care of me, you could see him with your own amber eyes.

"Thanks for coming," I said to him.

"How do you feel?"

"Awful."

"Let's get you home."

I whispered so the receptionist couldn't hear me: "I still haven't heard from him."

"Let's get you out of here."

I lifted my head from Frank's chest and turned to leave. He held the door open for me. I said to the receptionist, "Thanks for all your help today," so she'd look over and see him holding the door, then watch us walk out together.

———

In the car, I dialed Derek's phone again. No answer. Left a message that said I was worried about him, that I hoped he hadn't left because of my behavior at Shawna's party and that we should reschedule soon with Dr. Montahugh to talk about all this.

I hung up and Frank said, "You don't have to worry."

"Where could he have gone?"

"You're bleeding," he said, leaning over to the glove compartment and pulling out a Kleenex. His car drifted into the next lane and someone honked. "Sorry," he said to the driver, too quiet for anyone besides me to hear, vaguely waving his hand toward the other car.

Then Frank's phone rang in his pocket. "No way am I answering that. I just got fired."

"What happened?"

"Long story."

"What's the short version?"

"They don't appreciate my artistic contributions."

"Why?"

"That's the long part."

I took the Kleenex from his hand and wiped my mouth, mumbling, "I'm pretty sexy, huh?"

Second ring.

Frank smirked and said, "Who doesn't love spit and blood?"

I smiled but stopped myself from holding it too long, didn't want him seeing my temporary teeth, not after the way the receptionist had stared at them. I ran the Kleenex over my lips again. I tongued the back of the bridge. There was no way I'd ever get used to the way this felt.

His phone rang for the fifth time.

"What if it's Derek?" I said.

"It's not."

Sixth ring.

"How do you know?"

"It's probably friends from work calling to hear my side of things." His phone stopped ringing.

I wanted to yell at Frank. I wanted to tell him to look at what I'd done to my teeth, what I'd done to my whole face. Wanted to remind him that I'd just had my teeth drilled to bits, and if I wanted him to check his phone and make sure it wasn't Derek calling, why not give me what I wanted after all that had gone wrong?

"Where is he?" I said.

Frank exhaled and rubbed his nose. "I don't know." His phone started ringing again. He still didn't reach for it.

"You haven't talked with him?" I said.

Third ring.

"No."

"Since when?"

"Since… you… fell."

Fifth ring.

Frank pulled his car through two lanes of traffic and stopped in front of a liquor store, flipping on his hazards. "Do you want anything?" he asked. "I just got fired. I need a couple afternoon glasses of wine. I'll hang out with you until Derek's back."

"Really? Then grab two bottles. I want to get drunk."

He got out of the car with his phone still ringing.

FRANK:
THE UNVEILED ANIMAL

As I mentioned earlier, I'd been inventing a new kind of film-making called *The Unveiled Animal* (how it's germane to Derek and Mired's bizarre, sadistic tale will soon be clear, as will my plan for revenge against my brother). It revolved around the notion that the cinema needed to evolve past actors, scripts, contrived scenes, fraudulent emotion. Movies needed to shun closure and happy endings. There needed to be a convergence between mainstream filmmaking and documentaries. And with the blazing popularity of reality TV that developed in the late 1990s and early millennium, it seemed I might really be on to something. The public wasn't craving actors anymore, but people in real situations, real people who weren't pretending to feel sadness and anger and letdown but were learning to navigate the tangles and ignominies of everyday life.

Filmmaking, after all, is supposed to replicate voyeurism, and therefore the next logical step in its pubescent advancement would be to stop simulating life and actually capture it in the wild, in its raw environment, no soundstages or computer-generations. Film should record people in the midst of their naked days; it should embezzle the dread of human stagnancy and relay warnings to viewers, quiet cautionary tales denouncing complacency.

Derek and I had moved to San Francisco directly after high school. He worked at an auto parts store, and I was a film student at the Academy of Art and also had a part-time job as a production intern at an ad agency, long before Flo's narrow mind fired me. They let me use their digital film editing facility anytime I wanted, which was every evening I could feasibly get there, manicuring all the scenes I'd shot that week into some sort of freely cohesive narrative.

I spent literally all of my free time filming strangers, honing my eye as a director and cinematographer. I lurked in doorways, behind bus stops, sometimes trailed behind people or shadowed their movements from across the street – whatever I had to do to secure their particular scene(s). I was in training, preparing myself, because any day now I'd film the moment that would launch my career: the topnotch entertainment that would make the masses stampede to the box office.

And I'd been waiting. Patiently, for the first two years I was in my program at the Academy. Then I waited impatiently, intolerantly for the next two years, increasing my time out in the wild, sometimes wandering the streets all night hoping to stumble across the topnotch, a scene with enough danger to buoy a film. I tried to concoct compelling storylines with the material I recorded – I did the best I could with what I had – but at the end of the day, I needed that one eye-popping, sizzling image.

Each passing day grew harder to swallow, like a nest of gristle spackled in the back of my throat. Harder and harder to breathe with it wedged there. Each day tested my commitment to being an auteur.

Finally, the muse gifted me some of the topnotch.

I was in Golden Gate Park, near Hippie Hill, about ten p.m. It was freezing. Fog thick and wind rushing through the park from Ocean Beach. I was in the bushes filming a guy who'd grown angry with the drum he played and was now thrashing it to splinters. While he obliterated his instrument, a young woman, probably nineteen or twenty, walked through my camera's frame. She had dark skin, probably of Middle Eastern descent. She carried a book.

Golden Gate Park wasn't the most dangerous part of San

Francisco by any stretch, but it was an unspoken rule that women didn't walk through it at night, by themselves. *Why take the chance?* I'd heard women say over the years. *There are a lot of homeless men in the park. Why risk it?*

So what was this young woman doing? Where was she going?

I had to know. I let her get about thirty feet ahead of me, and I crawled out of the bushes. The guy who'd smashed his drum was now scooping its pieces up and putting them in his pocket, apologizing. His contrition, his explanation to the drum for why he'd dismembered it would have made a decent scene had this woman not come along.

I crept behind her, zooming in on her back as she bobbed in my camera's frame.

She wasn't walking very fast. The word *strolling* came to mind, and as we continued through the park, I thought of calling her section of my next film, *The Sad Stroll: a meditation on urban loneliness.*

And then she sat down on a bench. She opened her book.

I quickly dropped the camera to my side and walked past her, knowing somewhere ahead I'd find a place to skulk off the path and sneak up behind her so I could keep filming.

There was no light anywhere around her, which meant there was no way she could see the pages of her book. But she sat there, cross-legged, turning pages like she could make out the words.

I crawled through the bushes, stopping about fifteen feet from her. I pressed record and centered her body in the frame; it was an angle that captured her mostly from behind, a bit off to one side so I could see better, but that didn't matter. Head on, a profile shot, or the angle I had now, they all displayed the same thing: her vulnerability. She flipped the pages of her book faster, no way anyone could have read them, even if there was enough light.

It dawned on me: she wasn't really reading, just didn't have anywhere to go, didn't have anyone to spend time with. This was truly a meditation on urban loneliness! It took all my willpower to stay in the bushes. I wanted to jump out and tell her I knew exactly what she was going through. I knew how it felt to come home to an empty apartment, my only friend, my ridiculous twin, out drinking every night of the week until sunrise, staggering home and up our stairs and down our hallway and waking me as he spilled into the walls. I wanted to tell her that I knew what it was like to eat macaroni and cheese alone, how hollow it felt to masturbate myself to sleep. I could sit next to her on the bench and say, "You can tell me every single secret," and she would tell me something no one knew, she'd say something like, "I never read my fortune cookies because I can't take their pressure," and I'd say, "I've slept with the lights on my entire life," and we'd have this moment of recognition, a moment not divided by seconds or nanoseconds or minutes, we'd have a moment defined entirely by eye contact, staring and knowing that our individual solitudes were ready to rupture. We'd met another person who needed life to get easier. A person who understood the ruthless clamber of time as we worked our lives away in meaningless jobs. Someone who could empathize with feeling forlorn and weak.

And right when I wanted to hug this woman for the rest of my life, a man walked up to her and said, "You got the time?"

She didn't say anything, kept pretending to read the book.

He said, "Hey, you know what time it is?"

She said, "I'm not wearing a watch."

He said, "You got a cigarette?"

She said, "I don't smoke."

Then he pulled out a pistol and said, "Maybe you could lend me your credit cards. Would you like to lend me your credit cards?"

I stayed in the bushes, filming.

And I know how that sounds. I know that people are supposed to help one another. Under normal circumstances, I'd have leaped to her rescue. I hope you know that about me. I'm the sort of guy who believes in protecting others. For example: didn't I knock my brother to the ground when he refused to take Mired to the hospital and then drive her there myself? I've proven that I can act heroically when the situation demands it; however, as long as this woman did what the man said, emptied her purse of its valuables and didn't say anything confrontational, there was really no danger here. He didn't want to kill her. He was hungry or thirsty or withdrawing from drugs and needed money. That was it. Yes, he had a gun. Yes, he pointed it at her, but it wasn't like I had a weapon of my own, any means of combating his attack. I couldn't have done anything to defend her except put myself in harm's way, too. What would that have accomplished?

By now, he stood directly in front of her so I could see his front perfectly in my frame; he was dressed all in black, wearing a SF Giants beanie. He looked Latino, but I couldn't tell for sure. I kept the camera tightly fitted on their interchange.

"I don't have any credit cards," she said.

"Where's your purse?" he asked.

I sat up as stiff as I could, zoomed in all the way.

"I don't carry a purse."

He shook the pistol and said, "Empty your pockets, sweet cheeks. Before I get mad."

I knew she was scared – who wouldn't be scared with a gun in their face? – but in the long run, this was all going to be worth it. You wait for something your entire life and it falls into your lap and what are you supposed to do? Are you supposed to take your dream off the hook and throw it overboard, catch and release? Are you supposed to limp back to your cubicle and edit another batch of training videos, dousing your fluorescent wound with more salt? Why would I abandon this moment, this moment I'd waited so long for, all so some homeless tic could spend a week in county jail and be back on the streets, thieving from people who should know better than to sit in the middle of an urban park by themselves? Why should I forfeit the very thing that could change my life?

She stood up and turned out her pockets, handed him a small wallet.

"Anything else I'd be interested in?" he said.

"My cell phone?"

"A cell phone sounds enchanting. Thank you."

She took it out of her jacket pocket and handed it to him. "Please don't hurt me."

"Why would I hurt you?"

"Please."

"A pretty girl shouldn't sit in the park by herself. It isn't safe."

She didn't say anything.

He took a step toward her, gun still aimed square at her.

I couldn't zoom in anymore, so I extended the arm that held the camera, getting as close to them as I could without making any noise.

"I only want your money," he said to her, "but there are men around here who want more than that."

She fiddled with her closed book.

"I mean, what if I was one of those guys?" he asked and tucked the pistol in the front of his pants. "What then?"

She didn't say anything.

"It's your lucky night, sweet cheeks. I'm not one of those guys."

It was my lucky night, too.

Then he flipped his back to her, walking away, fast.

She sat on the bench for twenty more minutes, peering all around, even over both shoulders, with a look on her face I'd never seen. Fear? Relief that he'd let her live? Some amalgam?

Whatever her face's motivation, it was a wonderful expression, one with enough ambiguous character for a movie poster or the opening shot of a trailer. It was a look of subjective expression, rather than something easily categorized.

I couldn't believe my gigantic luck.

All my diligence had paid off.

I never took the camera off of her until she finally slunk away. I was freezing, but it was worth it.

MIRED'S DECIMATED HEART

Once Frank mentioned that he'd lost his job, I thought of getting fired from my last restaurant gig. I refused to apologize to an arrogant customer, who found my apathetic demeanor (his words) thoroughly unacceptable.

"I need you to say you're sorry," my manager said.

"But I'm not."

"Are you going to apologize?"

I hadn't made more than $150 in a shift for over a month. I wasn't willing to swallow my pride with that amount as compensation. "I don't think so," I said, and he let me go.

But even though I didn't care about the job, I was still upset. No one likes to be fired. No one likes to hear that they're not good enough. I called Derek and he said, "Come home, I'll take care of you," and as soon as I got there he said, "I'm in the kitchen."

He stood in the middle of the room, holding a baseball bat, a red *piñata* dangling from a nail in the ceiling, in the shape of a heart.

"What's this?" I said.

"Shhh," he said, coming over and handing me a vodka tonic. "We're celebrating your liberation." Then he walked behind me and covered my eyes with a bandana.

"Derek – "

"Just trust me."

And I did trust him.

He handed me the baseball bat, took my drink before I'd had a sip, which was something he'd normally never deprive me of. He turned me in a couple circles. I was dizzy. Derek said, "Swing, batter, batter," and I took a swing but missed it. He said the same thing again and I swung again and I missed again. "Help me," I said, and Derek took me by the shoulders and steered me toward the *piñata*. "Take all your frustrations out on the little bastard," he said, and I swung again, and this time I hit the heart, though it must not have been hard enough for Derek's liking, because then he said, "Pretend it's your old boss," and I hit it again, much harder, and he said, "Good. Now pretend it's your next boss!" I smiled. I swung again, connecting with the heart solidly, hitting it even harder. I heard a few things scatter on the linoleum. "Pretend it's everything in your life that's ever let you down!" he said and I did what most people do when they want to feel sorry for themselves: I thought of my parents: my dad who I never had the luxury of really knowing: my mom who didn't want the luxury of getting to know me, always busy gardening or volunteering or working a new part-time job for her *big cause!* of the moment, always exercising ("No one wants to look at a fat woman, Mired. No one. It isn't just men."), always dating, compulsively dating, until she met her new husband, her first since my father died over twenty years ago. And thinking about them – his corpse and her indifference – certainly helped me swing the bat the hardest yet, and I wanted to keep swinging; it felt good to keep swinging, as though each somehow ventilated, purged all the pent-up neglect and futility, and I must have finally crushed the *piñata* because of all the noises now clattering on the floor.

Derek took the bat from me, uncovered my eyes.

First I looked at the *piñata*, a decimated heart, tendrils of red crepe paper dangling from it like loose veins.

Then I looked to the floor, and there were white Jelly Bellys, coconut-flavored, my favorite candy, scattered all over. At the time, I remember thinking that they looked like shards of glass, but now, after all that happened, I guess it makes more sense to say they resembled teeth.

"I hope you're hungry," Derek said. "There are 200 Jelly Bellys here," and we lay on our stomachs, on the floor, eating all of them and sipping vodka tonics and laughing.

———

While I sat in Frank's car I kept thinking of the night I'd humiliated myself at Shawna's *Bon Voyage!* party. I'd sat in her kitchen and heard the other guests telling her how wonderful Cleveland was. I heard one guy say, "They've got a beautiful baseball stadium, that's for sure," and now with Derek missing and Shawna already in Ohio, I couldn't help but wonder if he'd fled to her. That he didn't want to be seen with my ugly, drooling, bruised face. That he wanted to be reunited in what I knew was a good relationship between them, but he denied it, always dismissing my instinct. I'm not talking about women's intuition: I'm talking about the way humans know obvious things, like whether they're in a humid climate or if they've been bitten by a dog.

I thought about him and Shawna. Cleveland. And I don't know why, but Cleveland's beautiful baseball stadium jarred itself in my brain: they'd have sex there, in dead center field, the stands full of spectators – voyeurs and vultures – cheering, masturbating, motioning to vendors for hot dogs and new sacks of peanuts. The stadium chock full of every person who'd ever let me down. A sold out show.

I wasn't even sure why I'd acted so wildly at Shawna's party or what made me so angry; I should have been giddy that she was moving far away from him. I should have kept my mouth shut. But I couldn't stop myself sometimes when I was drunk. Especially, when deep down there was a part of me that knew – there's a part of me that *still* knows – every aspect of life is seconds away from crumbling to pieces.

THE TWINS: MORE LORE

He'd come in our room and whisper: "The cobra's heart was supposed to dissolve inside me, from my stomach's acid and bile. But it didn't. It beat the whole damn day in the village. And I've felt it in me ever since."

"Is Mom still awake?" we said.

"Once the snake's heart slid down my throat, I could feel its predatory instinct take over. My blood went cold."

"Is Mom asleep?"

"It passed right into me, like it was contagious, like I'd always killed. The whole world became prey."

"Is Mom sleeping right now?"

"I'm trying to find an antidote, boys," he said. "You have to believe me. I know I need an antidote."

DEREK

Until you find yourself sprawled out on the floor, worrying that your girlfriend was about to rat you out to the proper authorities, you'll have to take my word for it that there's no word for it. Lousy thing was I couldn't find the keys to my truck, after getting up, searching everywhere. No surprise there, I guess. I was always losing my keys, couldn't keep track of where I threw them down. I even went out to my truck to make sure I hadn't locked them in there. No dice.

It was getting toward 5 a.m. Missing keys, at least, meant I couldn't drive to work. That took the situation down a pinch on the lousy-scale. Sure, I could have gotten there if I really wanted to, but why work if I could weasel out of it?

I called my boss. For thirty years he'd gotten to the garage at 4:30 in the morning. He always answered the phone by saying, "Speak to me." He liked to tell war stories about his younger, rugby-playing days, how he'd been such a badass before losing his leg in a motorcycle wreck and inflating to over three hundred pounds. But come on, I mean, how tough can you be if you buy your shoes one at a time?

"I've got the flu," I said, and he said, "Again, huh?" He wanted to fire me. I wanted him to fire me. But no matter our scorn for each other, I was good at my job and too lazy to find another, and Nick knew he'd have a hell of a time finding someone who worked on transmissions as fast as I did.

I decided to prepare for the worst because what were my

other options? Sit on my hands and act natural? Tell Mired the truth myself? There was no way I could do that. There was no reason to. It was a mistake, one lousy mistake, and there was no reason to ruin our life. It would never happen again and bringing it up to her would only make us fight when what we wanted, *what we both wanted*, was to become a better couple. We were seeing Dr. Montahugh and working on things. So if Frank came to his senses and minded his business and didn't open his trap to her, Mired and I could get our life back as long as she didn't know the truth. Everyone's always yammering on and on about how the truth is so necessary and important and basic, but I don't know – I think there's plenty we're better off being deaf to. I wouldn't want to know if Mired screwed somebody behind my back, and I could have done without all our old man's cobra-talk. How's this any different?

That was a big "if" about Frank anyway. Who knew what His Majesty the Narc was planning to do? I had no choice but to wait and see his next move.

My preparation for the worst included packing a duffel bag and taking $200 out of an ATM, and since I couldn't find my keys I waited until the car rental shop opened at six and got the cheapest one they had. I even asked about a GPS system, but the clerk yawned and stunk of booze and asked, "A GP-what?"

Talking to him reminded me that it was Mired who gave me the GPS for my truck; she always teased me about how often I was lost, saying things like, "You can barely find your balls with both hands." It was true, too, my sense of direction was lousy.

"Looks like my days of being lost are over," I'd said to her when she handed it to me.

"It will give you directions, sure." Then she stuck her tongue out at me. "But it isn't a miracle worker."

And speaking of directions, no one knew the route to make me laugh better than Mired. She could kill with one-liners. I don't mean giggling. I mean *hysterics*. I mean *intimacy*.

Back at the rental car agency, my phone rang. Frank. Calling from a payphone at the hospital because the battery in his cell had died.

Finally here he was with the dire information.

Finally I'd know the exact size of this impending lousiness.

"Mired's awake and wants to know why you're not at the hospital," he said.

"What did you tell her?"

"That you had to open the shop."

The bottom fell out of my brother's level on the lousy-scale. Plummeted from a perfect ten to a three. I didn't know why he was helping me, wondered if it had anything to do with us being identical: maybe he thought if he betrayed me and I went to jail, he'd have to see me every time he looked in the mirror, shaking my head at him, wondering how on earth you could do that to someone you're supposed to love? Didn't loving someone mean they deserved your devotion, no matter what?

"Thanks for helping," I said.

"She doesn't remember anything. You should come down here. They're putting a cast on her wrist. She's going to need a root canal later this week."

"Thanks for helping me."

"I'm not helping you."

"What are you doing?"

"I don't know," he said.

MIRED'S MUSEUM OF EMOTIONAL FAILURES

I never dated any exiles from the prestigious ilk. I knew that, knew none of my ex-boyfriends would ever cure a terminal disease or win a seat in congress. I didn't expect them to. But even the meek expectations I did carry with me were too much.

Exhibits A and B, selected at random from my lottery of dismal lovers, the male consolations we took home as sad prizes:

Exhibit A: the guy who urinated on my shoes. We'd been sleeping together for about a week. That night, we'd gotten drunk and passed out. I woke up and there he was, standing at my closet and peeing all over my shoes. All over ALL of my shoes: a sling-back pair of Franco Sarto's, suede Puma sneakers, Dansko clogs for when I waited tables, a pair of Bebe silver sequin pumps.

"What are you doing?" I said, and he said, "What?" and I said, "Are you going to the bathroom?" and he said, "Isn't this the bathroom?"

Days later, after I'd broken up with him, he had the insolence to call and say, "I left my coat at your apartment. Will you mail it to me?"

"Are you serious?"

"It's my favorite."

"I'm keeping your pea coat," I said, "as payment for all my pee-shoes."

Exhibit B: the guy I'd dated who came out of a stall in a women's bathroom with some other girl. I said, "What are you doing?" and he said, "We were only doing coke," and I knew that if a man ever, ever confessed to doing drugs as his alibi, then he was much guiltier than I'd initially alleged.

There are more of these pathetic exhibitions from my museum of emotional failures, all the men that line the grounds of my psyche like paintings or sculptures. The men that decorate my past, decorate my present, probably decorate scenes of my life that haven't even happened yet.

———

Frank got back in the car and handed me the brown paper bag. It was heavy.

"What else did you buy?" I asked.

"I got three bottles of wine. Just in case."

"Just in case what, we get snowed in?"

"In case we remember what we're trying to forget," he said, pulling the car back into traffic.

"Did you check your messages?"

"I didn't have any messages."

"Did you check your missed calls?"

"No."

"Would you mind checking for me, so I know if it was Derek?"

"Fine." He kept driving, didn't make any effort to pull his phone out.

I stared at him.

He looked back at me. "You mean right now?"

"Please."

We were at a red light. He arched his back and dug in his pants pocket for his phone, flipping it open. Pressed buttons. Then he shook his head and said, "No Derek."

I didn't believe him. "Who was it?"

He shut the phone and worked it back into his pocket. "A coworker. An ex-coworker."

"Can I see?"

"You don't believe me?"

"I just want to know who called."

"I told you."

I didn't say anything.

"Do you want me to show you it wasn't Derek?"

"I'm sorry," I said, lisping, exhausted, face still numb, worried I'd finally scared Derek away; for all our problems that was the last thing I wanted. "It's been a long week."

———

Frank and I pulled up to the apartment building. Derek's truck wasn't there. I was getting some of the feeling back in my face and wondering if I should call the police. But I decided to give him the rest of the day to show up before I involved the cops.

We lived on 20th street, between Valencia and Guerrero in the Mission district. While our apartment building was adorable on the inside – plants lining the shared hallways, a claw-foot tub, great hardwood floors in every room except the kitchen and its hideous yellow linoleum – the outside was a travesty. It looked like a 1950s motel or a funeral home. A concrete walkway running around the perimeter of the building, cheap stucco walls. We never liked the way it looked, but the inside outweighed the rank exterior.

Now sitting in Frank's car all I saw when I looked at it were the stairs, those teeth-stealing stairs, each step a reminder of how pathetic I'd become.

Frank got out of the driver's side; I sat there for a minute, staring at them, pushing my tongue against the numb fake teeth.

He came around and opened my door. "Are you okay?"

"I still can't believe it."

"He'll turn up."

"Not Derek," I said. "I can't believe I fell."

Frank extended a hand and helped me out of the car; I handed him the bag of wine bottles. It was late afternoon now. The wind was worse. The fog getting thicker, wetter. I was so cold. I was so pathetic. We approached the stairs, and as we stood at their bottom, I got light-headed; this had happened every time since my accident: I'd get close to them and suddenly feel as though I might collapse in a fit of culpable vertigo: being at the epicenter of my greatest failure was too grand a burden to endure. They made me feel guilty, dirty, worthless, disappointing. And the fact that I was relatively young didn't matter, didn't hatch the tiniest respite. Why would being young matter if I'd proven time and again too dense to learn from my mistakes?

I looked down to see if there were any pebbles of my teeth scattered on the sidewalk, but I didn't see any rubble. I took a deep breath. "I did it right here," I said, almost crying, pulling lightly on my upper lip, a habit of nerves that I'd had since childhood.

We'd only taken a couple steps up when Frank said, "Don't worry. You'll get new teeth and everything will be great."

"I don't want fake teeth. I want mine."

When we reached the top of the stairs, I stopped and looked back down them, trying to remember anything from that night. Trying to remember one fleck of detail as to what had happened, but I couldn't recall anything. It was painful to realize that I could maul my entire face, my entire life, and not have one tattered memory.

"These new teeth will be yours," Frank said.

"You know what I mean. I want the teeth that grew in my mouth."

"Sometimes we need replacements," he said with optimism, real optimism. He was lucky enough to see joy in fakes and prosthetics. I wasn't so lucky. Intellectually, I knew that they were here to help our injured lives, but all I saw was what they'd replaced. I saw the missing. I saw damage. Detritus. Crumbs.

DEREK

When I got to the emergency room, the admittance nurse told me to take a seat and that Mired would be out shortly. Question was whether I'd still be sitting there because of the two security guards eyeballing me, standing over in a far corner with a look in their eyes like Frank-the-narc had aired my dirty laundry. The guards reeked of hangovers and alimony payments and steroids and insomnia and I was getting lousy with nerves, but then they left through a set of double doors and never came back.

Frank was gone. No way to get a hold of him since he didn't have a landline and his cell phone was dead. I rifled an issue of *Newsweek*, zipping through the whole magazine, never reading a word, never spending more than two seconds on any particular page. I picked up another *Newsweek*, did the same thing. Flipping fast. Pictures blurring together. The faces. Congressional faces. Important international faces. Faces of American soldiers in desert camouflage. Faces of Iraqi insurgents. I liked how they all melded together the faster I flipped.

Then Mired came out, a nurse pushing her in a wheelchair.

My eyes fixed on Mired's face. The only one that mattered. The one I'd sabotaged.

Her right eye had blackened. The swelling had closed it to a slit, like a permanent wink. Just like our old man used to do: winking, his tepid affection, before he vanished. Mired's broken arm lay in her lap. Some stitches on her forehead. They'd cleaned all the scrapes on her face to shiny welts, but soon they'd scab over.

It was weird, seeing her like that. I hadn't really thought about what had happened. I'd been too preoccupied about going to jail, but seeing her smashed face made my stomach tingle, like I was suddenly starving.

"You got off work?" she said, slurring her words, wrecked teeth whistling a bit when she talked.

"I wanted to make sure you were okay."

Mired smiled. Just a little. Lips curling slightly at the corners. You could tell it hurt her.

I looked at the nurse. "Ms. Pelayo is on pain medication," the nurse said, butchering the pronunciation of Mired's last name. The nurse, like me, was another Caucasian confused by Filipino vowel sounds. "Take her home and put her straight to bed."

"She's in good hands," I said, then went to pull the car up, got Mired out of the wheelchair, and helped her into the passenger seat.

She's in good hands: what was I talking about?

"Whose car is this?" Mired said.

In the midst of everything, I'd forgotten about it. "It's a rental from the shop by my work," reaching across her lap to fasten the seatbelt. "I was rushing to get to you and couldn't find my keys. Truck's still at home."

"You couldn't borrow one from the garage?"

"None are running right."

She gave me another one of those tiny smiles that seemed to cause her so much pain. "I'm glad you're here," she said.

For the first time, I felt guilt, my torso going nuts like I was being eaten from the inside out. Something dining on my entrails without pity. Something stinking of purpose and haste. I'm sure I'd felt guilty for things over the years but never like this, nothing like this. A feeling of utter consumption.

MIRED

I stopped along the walkway to check the mail; any distraction, even something this trivial, was helpful, welcome. Frank stood next to me, holding the wine. It was the normal junk – advertisements, Derek's cell phone bill, another threat from the IRS – but there was also a summons for jury duty.

"Anything good?" Frank asked me.

I showed him the summons. "My civic chore."

"That's no fun."

"It's ridiculous," I said, because who was I to cast a vote on someone's guilt or innocence? How was I qualified to weigh in on somebody else's life when my face was still numb from Novocain, fake teeth roosting in my mouth? Shouldn't you demonstrate the tiniest tremble of competence before they dole any authority to you?

A jury of your peers.

A blurry haze of fears.

A fury forms your tears.

FRANK GETS THE TRUE TOPNOTCH

I decided that maybe I should keep filming the bench where that girl had been robbed. It had been the setting for the most topnotch footage of my career so how could it hurt to spend some more time there? Either I'd get another dose of brilliant material or I wouldn't. No harm done.

I spent six days, crouching in the bushes, feeling the wind's brutish strength, eating Power Bars, only finding benign things to film. I'm sure it sounds boring, but even the mere insects of possibility that I might get another blast of topnotch entertainment kept me satiated in the bushes, ecstatic in the bushes, totally thrilled.

And then it happened.

The unimaginable happened.

She came back.

She, the same she, who a week earlier had been robbed at gunpoint, came back to the same bench and pulled out her book (I couldn't tell if it was the same book), pretending to read.

Yeah, it was night, sure, it was dark, but you have to trust me, it was her. I'd watched the footage so many times I would have recognized her anywhere.

I pulled my camera out, wedged her in the center of the frame, the same angle as before, behind her and to the side. My mind tumbled possibilities: had she come back for revenge? Did she have her own gun? Was she bait, and the police were hiding all around, waiting to charge? Whatever the answer, I knew that

I was about to get another dose of the topnotch. I could already hear critics and scholars dissecting my contribution to international cinema, could hear my mom say to me, "My little Kubrick, my young Coppola," could imagine interviews and speeches at university film departments across the country, cocktail parties at Cannes and Venice and Sundance film festivals, imagine sitting in a tuxedo at the Oscars, the buzz of the paparazzi as they toted me and the significance of my work, *the most major leap since early Lynch!* as I had the guts and verve to stitch together real life and film. And maybe I'd invite this young woman to be my date, my leading lady, maybe she and I could do the talk shows together: genius and muse.

She kept flipping pages.

And then it happened.

The unfathomable happened.

He came back, too.

He, the same he, who a week earlier had robbed the young woman at gunpoint, marched right up to her again. He was wearing the same outfit, the same beanie, might have been Middle Eastern himself instead of Latino. He stood with the same posture, letting the déjà vu of his words seep from his mouth, asking her, "You got the time?" and, just like last week, she didn't answer him, feigning a willed interest in her literature, actually flipping a page with him standing there, in defiance of his intrusion, refusing to look up at him, at his brazenness, his tactlessness, his aggressive pose, and he said, "Hey, you know what time it is?" and she said, "I'm not wearing a watch," and he said, "You got a cigarette?" and she said, "I don't smoke."

And right on cue, in the same exact moment as last week, the guy pulled out a pistol. And right on their cues, with the precise reproduction of everything I'd witnessed last week, these two people reenacted their scene to perfection, ending with him fleeing, while she sat on the bench, while I huddled in the bushes, filming, astonished, confused.

When I got home from filming the same man robbing the same woman in the same place, I ran into our apartment and said to Derek, "You won't believe this."

He was eating a burrito, drinking a Negra Modelo, watching an old Bill Murray movie on TV. "Did you finally catch some teenagers screwing in the park?"

I fiddled with my camera, hooking it up to the TV, interrupting Bill Murray in the midst of another predictable one-liner.

"I was watching that," he said.

"You have to see this."

"Later."

"I filmed two armed robberies."

He lit up. "*Adios*, Bill Murray. Why didn't you say so?"

I pressed play, and we watched the one from last week, Derek not saying a single syllable while viewing topnotch material from *The Unveiled Animal*; Derek, who couldn't stop from giving his running commentary on everything in life, sat there, speechless, his mouth moving only to make a smile when the guy whipped out the gun, and after the scene ended, Derek said, "Cool," and I said, "That's nothing."

The TV screen was black, six seconds of dead time between the two robberies, and if my brother was any indication, my first guinea pig into mass response of *The Unveiled Animal*, the world of mainstream filmmaking was about to turn upside-down, like when Pollock started dripping paint all over his canvasses, instead of doing what he'd been told, what he'd been spoon-fed for his whole preceding career: *People paint with brushes!* It takes people like me and Pollock, people who see accepted conventions as nothing but invitations to shove the boundaries, to shove them so far that they stop indicating restricted zones. They transcend these divisions. They evolve.

Or maybe they devolve. Maybe devolution is a better way to think about it, as they shed the codes of their previous existences.

They devolve from Homo Erectus to apes to frogs to fish. They lose their ability to take breaths of our atmosphere. They crawl back into the ocean. They are shapeless young creatures, struggling to identify their characteristics, to define their nascent species. They are the beginning of new life. New eras. Maybe there's no difference between evolution and devolution if they both lead to change.

The six seconds were up, and the next robbery started to play on the TV, the woman walking up to the bench, sitting, opening her book.

"That's the same chick," Derek said, taking the last sip of his Negra Modelo, opening another bottle.

"I know it is."

"You filmed her getting robbed twice?"

I nodded and smiled at Derek.

It took a couple seconds for this possibility to sink in as vaguely plausible, and then he said, "This is unbelievable," and I looked back at the screen, still smiling, still in awe of my luck, saying, "It really happened, so it's believable." We watched the rest of the scene in silence. Then the screen went black again. Derek opened another beer and handed it to me.

"Congratulations," he said, and we touched the giraffe-necks of our beer bottles.

More quiet.

"This is what you've been waiting for," he said. "What do we do now?"

"We?"

"You know what I mean."

"I guess I'll go back next week and hope to see them again."

"And then?"

"I don't know."

"I know," he said.

"What?" but I didn't really want to hear one of Derek's crackpot plans about life. Yet I couldn't just dismiss or ignore his wild ideas, either, because *The Unveiled Animal* was born from people's savage compulsions. Our inexplicable chaos. Our desperation. Our ingenuity for creating new means of arrogant betrayals. Our animal is constantly swindled by its appetites.

"It's a game," Derek said. "Their fetish."

Honestly, I hadn't really thought about their motives for the faux-robberies, too immersed in my fantasies about *The Unveiled Animal*'s extraordinary future to worry why this couple met in the park to fake a crime. "What's their fetish?"

"The same one we all have," he said, standing up now and using his arms as visual aids, waving them in huge circles. His beer foamed and leaked out of the bottle's tip. He wiped it on his jeans. "We're bored to death and need excitement. We need to tempt fate, need to feel our endorphins kick like babies. We need to know we're still alive."

I laughed, sipped my beer, shook my head at his untamed theory.

He was still standing, but his arms were at his sides. "You should think about it."

"Think about what?"

"What I'm suggesting."

"What are you suggesting?"

"The element of surprise," Derek said.

"Surprise?"

"Yeah."

"You want to rob them?"

"I want to present the illusion of genuine criminal intent."

"What?"

"If they're looking for adrenaline," he said, "we'll give them adrenaline."

MIRED: STAINED WITH A VAGUE SORROW

Exhibit C: a few years back, my hair was really long and I was dating a white guy with dreadlocks to the middle of his back. One night we drank a whole bottle of tequila and I blacked out. Here's the story as he told it to me later (and, by all means, take his version of the evening as nothing more than another bouquet of lies): "We decided to shave each other's heads, babe, and then, you know, I shaved your head."

Those were his ludicrous words.

I can't tell you exactly what happened that night, after, say seven or eight shots of tequila, but I can tell you that I woke up the next morning, on the bathroom floor, surrounded by dunes of my hair and I stood up and looked in the mirror, completely bald and started bawling, and the guy strutted into the bathroom and said, "What's wrong?" and I said, "Look at me," and he told me what I just told you – that we stayed up and shaved each other's heads. Then I said, "But you still have all your hair," and he said, "You decided not to shave mine," and I said, "Why did I decide that?" and he said, "Because you love my dreads so much," and I said, "I love my hair a lot more than I love yours," and he said, "That's what you said," and I said, "Liar!" and he said, "No, really, that's what you said," and I said, "You liar!" and he said, "Really," and I said, "Then let me shave it now," and he said, "What?" and I said, "Let me shave your head right now!" and he said, "Calm down," and I said, "Let me shave it!" and he said, "Seriously, you didn't want to shave my head," and I said,

"Seriously, I want to shave it right this second."

Our argument made him flee the apartment.

Afterward, I swept all my hair up in a dustpan.

———

Frank and I walked in the apartment and sat at the kitchen table. Our whole kitchen was filthy. Piles of dirty dishes teetered on the counter, boomerangs of pizza crust on the top plates. Three empty bottles of vodka sat in the sink, next to the coffee cups we drank vodka tonics out of, brown limes like snails shriveled in the bottoms of the mugs.

Frank uncorked the first bottle of wine and poured us both big glasses. "What should we drink to?" he said.

"To living on the first floor in my next apartment."

He laughed. I tried to fight off laughing, tried to hold my lips together, though I couldn't, exposing my hideous bridge. I didn't want Frank examining how awful the teeth looked.

It was weird looking at someone identical to my lover, especially when my lover vanished when I really needed him, and here was his brother, a perfect doppelganger, an imposter in the best sense of the word: an understudy proving to be more gifted than the leading man, a prolific replacement. Because what kind of leading man disappeared during a big show?

"I've got a surprise for you," he said, walking over to the counter and opening the brown bag that had the rest of the wine. He pulled out a red rose. A fake red rose. "I bought it at the liquor store. I know it isn't the real thing, but I wanted to get you something."

I took the fake rose from him; the petals were made of plastic. "It's beautiful."

"Well, you're handling all this beautifully," he said.

"I don't know about that," I said, forgetting for a second that it was fake and smelling the rose. I immediately blushed because I was used to Derek and he would have made fun of me for sniffing a fake flower; but Frank asked if he could smell it, too, and I held it out to him and he took a huge gulp of air into his lungs, saying, "Perfect."

I brought the flower back up to my nose and nodded at him, *perfect*.

"Should I put it in water?" he said and smiled at me. "We don't want it to die." He laughed again. Then he took a pint glass from the cupboard, placed the fake rose in it, and set it on the windowsill behind the kitchen sink.

Derek hadn't given me flowers – real or fake – the entire time we'd been together.

"Will you open that window a bit?" I said. "I could use the fresh air."

———

Half an hour later. Half an hour of sipping wine. We were on the second bottle. Half an hour of me staring over at the fake rose on the windowsill. There was a bumblebee buzzing around it, landing on the plastic petals and sticking its head inside, looking for nectar. When the bee didn't find what it wanted, it would buzz around the rose some more. It must have been so confused: it had done this a thousand times, extracting what it needed from a thousand different flowers, but not this one, not this time.

I remember seeing on Animal Planet that bumblebees shouldn't be able to fly. Something to do with their wingspan versus their body mass. It was why they flew so herky-jerky, clumsily bounding every which way; they flew like babies learning to walk. But they could fly and the reason was simple: they didn't know that what they were doing was impossible. They didn't know the laws of motion and force. They had wings, and they used them. Simple as that.

It was strange to think how much your life could change when you weren't paying attention. One minute, you had a father, you had a mother who wasn't too busy to be bothered, you had teeth, you had a boyfriend, and you blinked your eyes, one quick blink, and by the time you looked around again, your whole life was stained with a vague sorrow.

———

I told Frank that I needed to go to the bathroom, but really, I wanted to write in our couple's journal. It had been recommended by Dr. Montahugh. When situations got volatile, Derek and I were supposed to write our feelings down without getting defensive or fighting or blaming. We kept it by the bed. The journal's cover used to have the pictures of the Greek masks for comedy and tragedy, but Derek had scribbled over the comedy one, blacking it out completely. Guess what that left us?

I wrote: *I have to change. You have to change. Can you do that?*

I should have written in pencil. Montahugh said not to use the word *you* in the journal. "Write with I-statements," she'd said. "I feel this, I feel that. No accusations."

I ripped the page out of the journal, crumpled it up, threw it on the floor. I tried to start over, but I couldn't find a way to word it without using *you*. I was too used to blaming him and didn't know how else to detail our deficiencies.

In retrospect, maybe the word *we* would have accomplished the task, conveyed unity amidst the knowledge that there was so much work for us to do. But retrospect isn't worth anything; it's just a fancy word for self-hatred and second guessing; it's lingering shame.

From the street, I heard a construction worker fire up a jackhammer. That terrible blare of buckling asphalt. San Francisco had been tearing up and repaving this street since Derek and I had moved in, something to do with the sewer lines. At the end of every week, it seemed like the workers were finished, and they paved the street black and smooth. But the following Monday morning, they ripped it open again, always gouging the same spots.

Whenever I heard the jackhammer I yearned to live in the country, wished my dad was still alive, that I really knew what he was like before the cancer. That I had more memories of him before he was sick. I do remember that his family always threw the most amazing parties. We'd show up late to Aunty's place (Dad was always late). The women would have made too much food, *rellenong bangus* and *pancit*, and we'd wash it all down with cup after cup of *sago*; the men drank scotch mixed with 7UP and bragged to one another; the kids, mesmerized by the video games, ate huge bites of milk fish when it wasn't their turn to play.

I'd settle for hearing one rotten bird sing right now, but as I stared out the window, the only trees I saw were telephone poles, the only bird an urban woodpecker: the jackhammer slamming its metal beak into the road.

DEREK

When we pulled into our apartment building after leaving the ER, Mired was asleep. I carried her up the stairs. Did you hear me?

I carried her up the stairs.

I carried her up the stairs.

I carried her up the stairs.

I carried her up the stairs.

MIRED

I'd been afraid when I lost my first baby tooth because I didn't believe that another would grow in its place. My dad tried to reassure me, opening his mouth wide and saying, "Every tooth fell out of my mouth when I was a kid and look at all these chompers."

"How can I eat if all my teeth fall out?"

"They don't fall out all at once."

"What if mine do?" I said.

"My *inay* taught me to make the best *sopa de fideos* and if your teeth fall out, you can eat it at every meal."

"Grandpa taught you?"

"We need to work on your *Tagalog*."

Later that week I lost another tooth and was convinced all my teeth were falling out and none would ever grow in my empty mouth. I said, "I don't want to lose my teeth," and he said, "Your new ones will be bigger and stronger," and I said, "What if they're not?" and he said, "Would you like some *sopa de fideos?*" and we cooked together and I didn't know anything about his tumors yet, and I wish he were alive to make me soup today; I wish we could cook together and talk and he could give me advice, could help me learn about myself, that side of the family. I needed a teacher, an advocate. Because the only thing I knew about being half-Filipina were the cuss words.

DEREK'S TERMITES FEAST
ON RANSACKED GUTS

Got Mired in bed, turned the TV to Animal Planet, Mired's favorite channel. Some guy was holding a hula-hoop and a cat jumped through it. I asked if she wanted anything to eat, but she said there was no way she could hold food down yet.

"What do you actually remember?" I said.

"Just Shawna's party," she said. "Making a fool of myself."

"You didn't."

"I feel terrible."

"Do you want your earplugs?" I said, but what I really wanted was for someone to give me a pair of my own.

She nodded and said, "I love you."

I stuck the plugs in her ears and kissed the side of her head and lay down next to her. I said, "I love you, too," but knew she couldn't hear me.

————

After a while, I got a feeling like there were termites working their way through my body, decimating anything they could sink their teeth into. I could feel them crawling around and chewing me to splinters, and I told Mired that I loved her, even though I knew she couldn't hear me and the termites scavenged my body, and I was lying right next to her, trying to sleep, trying to calm down, but I couldn't calm down because she was right here, a battered reminder of the man I'd turned into. *She's in good hands.* I never wanted to be this person, never wanted to be some terrible sadist with his temper mauling the world, I wanted to be better than that, better than our old man, but I'd done it, it was already done, I'd dropped her and turned into a terrible sadist with termites chopping me up, and Mired was snoring a little with her earplugs deep and she didn't know what I'd done and I knew what I'd done, I knew exactly, could still feel my arms straining to carry her weight up the stairs and every awful thing she said, the names she called me, it was like Mired hated me or why was she saying those things? and the termites gutted me and all I could do was cry and say, "Sorry, sorry, sorry," and I kept crying and she kept snoring and I was saying, "Sorry, sorry," and I couldn't sleep and I put my palm on my chest to feel my heartbeat, and all I could do was wonder how I ended up being the kind of person who did something like this, how I ended up being the lousiest turd in the world, hurting the person I was supposed to love.

———

When I woke up, Mired was still snoring. We'd fallen asleep with the TV on, and now there was a show about hammerhead sharks.

The voice-over said, "Hammerheads have a violent mating ritual."

There were hundreds of sharks paired up, all slowly falling through the water.

The voice went on to describe how a male shark grabbed and nipped and bit the female, using his jaws to make her submit, holding on to her with his jaws as he shoved his penis inside, holding on no matter how she tried to fight him off. They copulated as they floated in the water, slowly sinking toward the bottom because neither shark swam during sex. The male held on to her until he was finished. Sometimes they sank all the way and landed on the ocean floor. Sometimes the male finished before they reached the bottom and the female swam away from him as fast as she could.

Watching them mate was beautiful. It really was. Yeah, I know it doesn't abide by what we think of as "consensual," with all our sophistication and liberal arts colleges and atomic bombs. But I dug watching them paired up and sinking together.

———

I dozed again. When I woke up and looked at the clock, it was noon. I got up to take a shower but when I started to make my way to the bathroom, Mired said, "Don't leave." She said it loud because her earplugs were still in.

I got back in bed and took the plugs from her ears.

"Do you need something?"

"My teeth," she said. "I need my teeth. I can't believe I did this to myself."

Termites gnawing on my spleen, left ventricle, carotid artery, thigh fat. It was the worst feeling of my entire life.

"I'm so ugly," Mired said.

"You are not."

"My teeth are gone, and it's my fault."

"Don't say that."

"Are you mad at me?" she said.

"Why would I be mad at you?"

"I'm sorry about the party. Don't give up on me."

"Why would I give up on you?" I said, stunned. More ravenous termites sawed their way through my vocal cords and I couldn't say a word. I was supposed to soothe her but couldn't do anything except lie there and be eaten alive.

"Shawna's," she said. "I'm so embarrassed."

The termites finally pulled their fangs from my vocal cords. "You should rest."

"Did I embarrass you?"

"Of course not."

"I'm so ugly," she lisped, and I told her, "No, don't say that, you look perfect," and she said, "Don't lie to me," and I said, "No really, you look perfect," and she said, "Don't lie," and asked me to hold her, so I took her in my arms. I did my best to calm her down, rocking her, making shushing noises, but no matter what I tried, she was inconsolable.

"Do you want some soup?" I asked.

Mired said no, but I insisted, telling her she hadn't eaten much dinner last night and her body needed some fuel, it had been through a lot. I told her to rest and put her earplugs back in.

"Thanks for taking such good care of me," she said, too loud because of her clogged ears.

———

Frank called while I put the soup on the stove, using one of the back burners because the front ones were busted. "How is she?" he said, not waiting for me to answer before blurting, "You have to tell her the truth."

"Now hold on."

"If you don't, I will."

I knew Mired couldn't hear me from the other room, but I whispered anyway. "And just what are you going to tell her?"

"That you threw her down the stairs."

I'd been telling myself for months that I didn't deserve Mired's jealous frenzies, wondering why she didn't trust me since I'd never given her any reason to question my loyalty, but I finally had. I'd given her a great reason, the golden reason.

"That's not the kind of thing you tell someone unless you know for sure," I said.

"Well, *you* do know for sure."

I wanted to dump some of Mired's soup in a bowl, but I needed both my hands to pour it. Tried to tuck the phone between my shoulder and ear. It slipped and fell to the floor. By the time I picked it up and said, "Are you still with me?" Frank had hung up.

———

"Here's your soup," I said to Mired.

"What?" She took her earplugs out.

"Soup."

It was obvious she didn't want any, but she let me spoon it up to her lips. Mired only had like six slurps before she said she was full. Something was better than nothing, I figured.

"We need to call a dentist," Mired said.

"Do you want me to do that now?"

She nodded. "I want to get this fixed as soon as we can. Do you think people will be able to tell my front teeth aren't real?"

I pushed another spoonful of soup up toward her mouth, and she frowned at me, but I didn't care, holding it there until she sucked it down. "No way."

"Really?"

"They'll be better than the real thing," I said, guiding the spoon to her.

She shook her head and scowled. "Why did you call Frank after I fell?"

"I'd agreed to open the shop for Nick, and he'd have fired me if I didn't show up. So I figured Frank could take you to the ER and I'd meet you there as soon as Nick got in." I pointed the spoon at the soup. "A little more?"

Mired rolled her good eye but agreed to eat some more. "Why did he need you to open?"

My hand shook so much that as I brought more toward her face, I spilled on our comforter. "Damn." I blotted it with a finger. "He had to pick someone up at the airport."

"How did you get to work without your truck?"

"Taxi."

"Sorry you had to rent that car, go to so much trouble." She tried to give me another one of those pitiful smiles.

"It's no trouble."

My cell phone rang. I put the spoon in the bowl and stood up to look at my phone. Frank. Sent it to voicemail.

"Who's that?" Mired said.

"Nick."

"Do you have to go back to work?"

"I'm not going anywhere."

"You'll have to call the restaurant for me," Mired said, "and tell them what happened. I can't wait tables looking like this."

"It might help your tips."

She winced and said, "Don't make me laugh." She brought her broken hand up to her face and rubbed her bottom lip. "Can I have another Codeine?"

I gave her a pill, which she washed down with a mouthful of tomato soup.

"And call Dr. Montahugh," Mired said, talking about our couple's counselor. She was the biggest termite of them all, and I knew she'd see right through everything and immediately know what I'd done. She'd say, "Derek, is there something you should tell Mired?" and I'd say, "No, ma'am," and she'd say, "I think we both know that you owe Mired an explanation," and there were no words that could ever defend what I'd done.

"Thanks," Mired said. "I don't want Dr. Montahugh to see me this way."

"I don't want her to see me either," I said.

———

Told Mired I needed to take a shower, but once the water was running and the bathroom door was closed, I called my voice-mail and listened to Frank's lousy message: *You could have killed her. She could have died. What would you have done then? Would you still have pretended like she fell? You would have. I know you would have. You're just like Dad. You have to tell her. She should know the truth.*

The bathroom filled with steam. Frank kept talking, saying that he was going to tell Mired himself if I wasn't man enough to do it. He said I could keep him from her today, maybe tomorrow, but one of these days he'd get through to Mired so she'd know who I was.

I dialed Frank's number. The bathroom was so steamy I couldn't see my face in the mirror, just a hazy shape standing there. It could have been anyone. I kept my message simple: "You're wrong about the truth. That's the last thing she should know."

FRANK: REINVENT THE WHEEL

The morning after Derek and I had watched the robberies and he'd suggested one of our own, he barged into my room holding two pint glasses full of a brown swirling liquid. He handed one to me.

I smelled it. "What's this?"

"An Irish Car Bomb," he said, telling me the ingredients: Guinness beer, with a few ounces of Jameson whiskey and Bailey's cream wading through its murk. "You're supposed to slug the whole pint right after dropping the booze in the beer. So drink it right now."

"What time is it?"

"A little after eight a.m."

"Isn't it early for an Irish Car Bomb?"

"You've never been to Belfast," he said, drinking his in a long gulp. "I did some film research online, and we need to talk about pacing."

"Pacing?"

"The pace of the scene. The way we're shooting it."

"I don't want this," I said, handing the Car Bomb back to him, which he happily slugged.

"I read that one of the major factors of a film's mood is its pacing."

"And?"

"And it's critical we create the correct rhythm."

"And what's that?"

"Since they do this out of boredom, I think our scene should be slow and gloomy. Paced to represent the neoplatonic interpretation of ennui."

"You don't even know what *neoplatonic* means."

"I don't know what *ennui* means either," he said, "but don't I sound like a filmmaker?"

———

I tried all sorts of halfhearted arguments to talk Derek out of doing this, tried saying, "The guy's got a gun."

"Why would it be real?" he said. "And if it is, why would it be loaded? He's only role playing with his old lady."

I tried saying, "What if someone gets hurt? What if something goes wrong?"

"What if? What if?" he asked. "Is there any more pitiful question in the English language?"

I tried saying, "What if these really are crimes? What if he's robbing her? Shouldn't we turn the tapes over to the police?"

Derek just laughed. He said, "I'd love to see you hand this over to the cops. Fork it over and say, 'Here, guys, here's the only chance for a future my measly career has. But why don't you take my movie as evidence. Good luck cracking the case. I'll sleep better tonight knowing you've stopped a couple kids from getting their rocks off in the park. By the way, do you know if any fast food joints in the area are hiring?'"

I tried saying, "How is this even going to work?" hoping he'd be dissuaded by having to formulate a plan, to actually think something through for once.

"Simple. You film. I act. The couple goes home and has the sex of their lives. We all get what we want."

"Wait," I said, "what's in it for you?"

"My secret."

"Tell me."

"Fine," he said. "For one night, I'll be the most important person in their lives. I'll be their hero."

"Hero might be overstating it."

"Maybe," he said, "or maybe when I stick a gun in their faces, they'll know that I could kill them if I wanted to."

"And that makes you a hero?"

"Hell, yes. I'll be the guy that lets them live. What's more heroic than that?"

———

The day I completely caved in and agreed to film the couple, I was at the agency. Flo was criticizing the way I'd cropped some interviews for a testimonial video. You could consider our bickering a precursor, a clue, as to the artistic argument that would lead to my firing.

"I need simple and clean," she'd said. "It's an internal video. No one will see it except our employees. There's no reason to spend time or energy making it conceptual."

"I just thought…"

"You thought that you'd" – Flo used air-quotes for the next three words – "'make it better.' We don't need better. We don't want to reinvent the wheel, Frank." Flo smiled at me, something she wasn't in the habit of doing very often.

"Okay." I nodded, slunk back to the editing room, and gave her the predictable boring, drivel she wanted. And afterward, I knew, without any doubt, that I had to go ahead and let Derek pretend to rob those people, had to start my real career or my whole life would simply be giving Flo her predictable, boring drivel over and over. This was my opportunity to capture a scene so compelling that no one could dismiss my talent or demean me with banal tasks.

Plus, Flo was wrong: I *was* here to reinvent the wheel. I am here to keep reinventing it. I called Derek on my lunch break and said, "I'm in."

He wasn't working at the auto parts store any longer, but at Nick's garage. "In what?"

"Let's make our movie."

———

We had a plan. I want you to know that. I want you to know that there was a plan.

MIRED

Exhibit D: there was the guy who tried to give me a curfew after we'd dated for three weeks. "A what?" I said, and he said, "I think you stay out too late," and I said, "I don't think you have any right to tell me what to do," and he said, "Well, if this relationship is going to work, I don't think you should be staying out half the night," and I said, "I don't stay out half the night," and he said, "Yes, you do. You're hungover every day," and I said, "I can do whatever I want," and he said, "Even if it's damaging our relationship?" and I said, "This relationship is over," and he said, "So it's more important to party than to be in our relationship?" and I said, "Go to hell," and he said, "Maybe it's time to admit you have a problem with alcohol," and I said, "Didn't I tell you to go to hell?"

———

I walked back into the kitchen and Frank said, "I need to tell you something."

We were still making our way through the second bottle of wine.

"What?" The bee kept circling the fake rose.

"But I don't know how to tell you."

"This will help," I said, tipping my wine glass up to my lips. Frank smiled and did the same. His smile was wider than Derek's. When Derek smiled you couldn't see his bottom teeth. I could see Frank's. "So tell me."

Frank set his wine glass down. "There's no easy way to bring this up."

"Just tell me."

"I can't just tell you."

"Why not?"

"Because – "

"Is it about me?"

"You and Derek."

"Is he leaving me?"

"I don't think so," Frank said.

"Where is he?"

"It's about the night of your accident." Then Frank's phone rang again. "Do you want me to check if that's Derek?" he asked.

"What were you going to tell me?"

Frank arched his back and pulled his phone from his pocket and shook his head. "Not Derek."

"Please tell me."

"Look," he said, holding his cell phone toward me, so I could see the caller ID. It said *Arianna*. "I worked with her."

"Finish what you were saying."

"I get fired for interjecting a bit of creativity. God forbid, we deviate from their precious template."

"Frank!"

"I'll leave my phone on the table, in case Derek calls."

"What were you going to say?"

He picked up his wine and took a sip. I took one, too. His nose was different than Derek's: his nostrils a little thicker, flared, like he was yawning all the time.

"Well, about your accident. Um. I. Um…" Frank shook his head. "Let me gather my thoughts."

"No! I knocked out my teeth! Derek is gone! If you know something, tell me!"

I looked over at the fake rose and the bee. I walked closer to them, over by the window; the urban woodpecker was gone, leaving only a huge hole in the road.

"Okay," he said, picking up his wine glass, drinking the whole thing, then picking up the bottle and taking a swig out of it, too. When he drank like that, he looked exactly like Derek. He stared in his lap and ran his hands through his hair, looking at me and pursing his lips. I couldn't be sure, but he had this awkward expression on his face, as if he was enjoying this. Enjoyed teasing this moment out to an absurd length. Titillated by the power of doling the information out in minute increments. Then he said, "You didn't fall down the stairs."

"What do you mean?"

"You didn't fall on your own."

Yes, there was no doubt now. Yes, Frank's face. He loved disseminating his covert news, loved delivering the devastating facts.

"I don't understand," I said.

"Derek was carrying you."

"No, I tripped."

"No," he said, "you didn't."

DEREK

I know the week went by, the days passing between me dropping Mired and when we finally went to the dentist – when I lost my mind with guilt and split town while she had her teeth fixed. I know the sun swung the earth around it like they were paired figure skaters. Or any other lousy, poetic shit that made science seem pretty.

I remember burning a grilled cheese and botching my sideburns that week.

Remember thinking our rent was late but not doing anything about it.

I remember insomnia. Haunting thoughts keeping me up while they yelled themselves hoarse like protesters. My own thoughts calling me disparaging names, the normal slang we slung to deface others. Asshole. Prick. Selfish bastard.

The worst one wasn't even profanity, but when I'd stare wide-eyed at the ceiling all sweaty and hear the protesters screech *you're your old man… you're your old man…*

But mostly I remember the termites. So many of them moving into me, more every minute, multiplying, stretching me, overcrowding and jockeying and writhing and thrusting their fangs. I'd burst. I'd die, if I didn't find a way to make them leave soon.

FRANK'S CHOIR OF MALICIOUS VOICES

And then pre-production was over, and it was time to film. Or time to go to the set, to get in the bushes and wait, wait and hope that the couple came back to the bench one more time. Time for Derek and I to huddle together, drink a couple beers, not too many, because I knew what could happen if Derek was drunk. We ate peanut butter sandwiches and Power Bars. We bundled up in beanies and jackets.

"This is brotherly love," Derek said.

For three nights we squatted in the bushes before it happened, before I saw my muse walking toward the bench, toward us, carrying her book. For the first time, I wondered what book it was. Was it a thoughtless prop, or had she selected it for a reason? I put my index finger up to my lips, exhaling. Derek nodded and whispered, "This is the moment we've been waiting for," and winked at me, like our dad used to, no hugs from him, never, just winks. Winks and his whispers and his head swelling with yelping voices from My Lai.

"Don't go until he's here, too," I said to Derek.

"I'm going to get a little closer and get into character."

"Just be quiet," I said, and he nodded and he walked a few steps toward the bench, still concealed by the bushes, but only fifteen, maybe seventeen feet from her. He pulled a pistol out of his jacket. It wasn't loaded. I put the camera up to my eye, pressed record. I was ready for my moment. I was excited, but as I saw her walk toward the bench, for the first time in all this, I got scared. Really scared. Petrified. Suddenly I felt like I needed to take a piss. She kept walking toward the bench, and I kept thinking how crazy it was that there were people in the world who didn't know how much they meant to us. This woman, this total stranger, was changing my life, and she didn't have any idea, had no concept of the influence she had over me, or how much influence my film would have in everyone else's lives. For a second, I loved her. Really I did. Not in a sexual way. I'm not some pervert. I loved her in the kind of way you love someone who was helping you. Can you imagine loving the person who saved your child from drowning? Can you imagine wanting to kiss the person who pushed you out of the way before a car could run you down? It was that kind of love, gracious and naked and pure. She sat down on the bench. I zoomed in on her. Derek held the gun. The gun wasn't loaded. Her black hair was shorter. It had been down her back before. Now it stopped at her shoulders. She opened the book. She flipped pages. Pages flipping fast. This was my moment. I was excited. I was scared. Derek wasn't looking at me, wasn't looking at her. Derek had his head tipped back. He couldn't see me, but I winked back at him. Tonight was the nicest thing my brother had ever done for me. I used to wonder why we were so different. We were fed the same food from the same woman in the same womb. How had we evolved into such different men? More pages flipping. It was cold outside, but I was sweating. Needed to piss. I liked her hair longer. The man marched up the path toward all of us. He was our savior, helping us get what we wanted. But while I loved her, I hated him. I don't know why. But I know that people can hate their saviors. Can have an animosity toward the righteous. Can despise how a savior's virtues expose our malnutritions. She wasn't flipping pages anymore. She was like me. Excited and scared. I knew it. I could tell. She crossed her legs. The man said, "What's a pretty girl like you doing all by her lonesome?" which wasn't in their previous script. Their game mutating. Perfect! I was thrilled. This was what I was trying to explain to you earlier about *The Unveiled Animal*: there was no way to predict real life, how people could deform patterns at a moment's notice. She said, "I'm waiting for someone." He said, "Can I wait with you?" She said, "No thanks." I kept the camera fixed on them. The frame was a little wider than the way I'd filmed them before so I could capture Derek's entrance. She turned a page in the book. She wasn't looking at the guy. He said, "Do you mind if I sit down?" She said, "Yes." He said, "It's not your bench." She said, "If you sit down, I'll leave." He said, "No, you won't." She said, "Yes, I will." He laughed. Laughed and slapped himself on the stomach. He sat down. He said, "What are you reading?" And then the rustling sound of a living thing, of an animal crunching through dried leaves. Derek. My twin. His body coming out of the bushes. The man, the woman turning to see him. Holding the pistol. It wasn't loaded. Derek storming up to the bench. Facing them. Facing the camera. It was a beautiful shot. Derek saying, "Put your fucking hands up." Them putting their hands up. Fingers extended. The woman saying, "Martin, what's going on?" The man saying, "Don't worry." Derek saying, "Shut the fuck up." Derek sticking the gun straight at the guy. The guy saying, "Okay, okay." The woman crying. Derek saying, "Shut the fuck up!" The man putting his arm around the woman. Pulling her against him. Shushing. Her crying dulling to whimpers. Me getting up off my knees and standing. Heart pounding. Derek saying to the guy, "Didn't you hear her say she didn't want you to sit down?" The guy saying, "It's not what you think." Derek saying, "What do I think?" Derek saying, "I'd be really curious to find out what I think." Derek saying, "Please go ahead and tell me what I think." Still pointing the gun at the guy. The gun wasn't loaded. I was getting less excited, more scared. Like the pistol was in my face. The guy saying, "This is my girlfriend." The woman saying, "We're just, you know, playing." Derek saying, "Playing?" Derek saying, "What are you playing?" The guy saying, "Please just let us go." Derek saying to him, "Shut the fuck up!" Derek saying to the woman, "Tell me what you're playing." Her whimpers revving back up to tears, shoulders shaking, saying, "Please." The guy crying now, too. The two of them, the singers inside their lungs belting out notes like a choir of malicious voices, some flat, some sharp, begging Derek in their ugly song. I tightened the shot so all I could see in the frame was Derek standing, and their shaking, scared shoulders. Derek saying, "What were you playing?" Her saying, "We were pretending." Derek saying, "Pretending what?" Her saying, "Pretending he was robbing me." Derek saying, "Why would you do that?" The guy starting to say something. Derek shaking the gun in his face to shut him up. The gun wasn't loaded. The woman saying, "I don't know why." Derek saying, "Think about it." She didn't say anything. Five seconds. Ten seconds. Fifteen seconds. Not a word. Great tension for my film. This was turning out better than I'd hoped. Derek saying, "You better fucking answer me." The woman saying, "We do it for fun," and crying harder. Derek asking, "Are you having fun?" Derek asking, "Is this a good time?" Derek asking, "Are you enjoying yourself or what?" The guy saying, "Please, sir." Derek saying, "You don't listen too good, do you?" and sticking the barrel of the gun against the guy's forehead. The guy saying, "Oh, Jesus." The girl sobbing like I'd never seen somebody sob. I wished I had a better angle to zoom in on her grief, to capture every streak streaming. And I should have been careful what I wished for, because right when I was wishing I could get closer to her sad face, Derek said, "Hey, Frank, why don't you come say hi to our new friends?"

What was he doing, what the hell was he doing, why was he using my real name? We never talked about me coming out of the bushes, all we'd discussed was me hiding and filming. Derek saying, "Frank, there's no reason I should have all the fun." I didn't know what to do. I didn't know what to think. Derek said, "Hurry up and get over here. I want you to see me shoot this guy in the head." New torrents of misery exploding from both of them. Derek with a heinous grin on his face. Was this the way our father grinned, slaughtering men, women, and children? Did he see the carnage and love the carnage? Was he sated with every bullet that sped from his rifle, every hole in a civilian's body? Derek saying, "Hurry up, Frank!" and I know I said I loved mutations, metamorphoses, improvisation, organic warps in trajectory, and that their unpredictability and chaos were imperative to *The Unveiled Animal*, but this wasn't what I wanted. This was the last thing I wanted. I wanted my eye to the camera and the camera on the actors. I wanted to capture the footage from the safety of a buffered vantage point. I didn't want Derek dictating the terms to me, didn't want him in control of my movie, not with his time-bomb temper. Not with his recklessness. Derek calling, "I'm waiting on you, Frank! Don't you want to see it up close and personal?" I wanted my body in the bushes and my eye to the camera and the camera on the actors and the footage being captured by your Reliable Eyewitness from the safety of a buffered vantage point. It didn't seem possible for me to get up, to follow his orders like he was my commanding officer, and I was to do what he said, no questions asked, I was to move toward them, toward him. It didn't seem reasonable or feasible or like anything I'd ever done. It was too risky and stupid. Too real. Too close. But I had to do it. I had to for the film's sake. Because right then, Derek's attention wasn't on the couple, it was on me, and if he didn't focus back on the scene's imperative momentum, we'd have done all this for nothing. It would be wasted. Done in vain and for naught. I'd be no closer to capturing the topnotch. I had to do what he said. I had to come out of the bushes. I had to. There was no choice.

Are you listening to me?

I walked out of the bushes and stood next to him, camera still at my eye, now facing the two of them on the bench. I widened the shot a little, so I could see both their woeful faces and

Derek's arm shoving the pistol right up to the guy's scalp. Derek said, "You're just in time to film me murdering this prick." The guy bawling. His eyes closed. The woman looking right at me and saying, "Please, please, please, please." Derek said to her, "Look in the camera and beg us." She did. "Please, please, please." Her bloodshot eyes. I zoomed in, framing only her face. "Please, please." Derek said to her, "Give me one good reason why he shouldn't die," and she said, "I love him," and Derek said, "Does that sound like a good reason, Frank?" but I couldn't say anything, lost in the smog of our ugliness. A lurching, sad knowledge spreading through me about what we were doing, who we were. "Please," she said. I fought back my own tears. You have to believe me that I had no idea what we were doing until that moment: her pleading into the camera, the gun to the guy's scalp. I knew we were going to scare them, but I didn't really know what it meant to truly scare someone. I didn't know anything until I saw her eyes looking into the camera and saying, "Please, please." I didn't know anything from the safety of the bushes but had to be in the village. I said to Derek, "Love is a good reason," and he said, "So I shouldn't kill him?" and I said, "No," and he said, "Are you sure?" and I couldn't do it anymore, I couldn't do anything, so I stopped filming, I turned the camera off and dropped the camera to my side. Walking away. Derek said, "Where are you going?" I didn't answer, crawling strides in the other direction. I heard him say to them, "Don't follow us. Sit here for fifteen minutes, or I'll kill you both." Then he ran up and grabbed me by the arm, said, "Come on. We have to get out of here," and we took off, sprinting through the park and catching a cab in the upper Haight and fleeing to our apartment.

THE TWINS: MORE LORE

Sometimes our old man would check us to make sure we were safe. "Let me feel it," he said to us. "I need to make sure I didn't pass it on to you."

"Feel what?"

"Lift up your shirts."

"Dad," we whined, knowing there was nothing we could do to stop him.

"Lift them up."

He checked us one at a time, putting his ear up to our stomachs, our chests, and listening. "I think you're all right," he said. "I only hear one."

FRANK: CLEAR MY NAME

You should have seen how happy Derek was, once we were home from filming them. He kept saying, "Did you see the panic on their faces? Did you see how much we scared them?"

The problem was I had seen their awful expressions: the guy's eyes squeezed shut, probably praying, the woman staring at the camera and begging us to stop. The only animals we'd unveiled were ourselves. Our lineage, our tainted bloodline.

You may not care anymore, after listening to me tell you what we did that night. But I want you to know that sometimes we don't know that what we're doing is wrong until after we've done it. It's one of our splendid calamities: we deceive ourselves until we taste the acrid consequences.

"Let's watch the tape," he said, carrying a six-pack of Negra Modelo and plopping on the floor in front of the TV. I was on the couch right behind him. He opened two of the beers and tried to hand one to me, but I shook my head. "Suit yourself," he said, holding a beer in each of his hands. He looked so thrilled with everything. "Time for the first screening."

"We ruined those people's lives."

"Don't be so dramatic," he said.

"My whole project is ruined. I can't believe you did this."

"Did what?"

"Ruined everything."

"How do you figure?"

"I wasn't supposed to come out of the bushes, Derek. That wasn't part of what we talked about."

"But you did."

"I didn't want to. I was supposed to film. That was all."

He drank one of the beers and set the empty bottle on the floor. "You knew exactly how far I was going to go. That's why you wanted me to do it. To push your movie to the limit."

"My movie is meaningless now. I can't show that to anyone. We'll go to jail."

"Just black out my face. Mute me using your name. No one will know it was us."

"I'll know it's us."

"Pathetic," he said. "It's pathetic that you want to back out now. Back out after we made the kind of movie you've been spouting off about for years. We made a movie of real emotion, Frank. Real people were scared for their real lives. You came out of the bushes, and now you want to scrap it?"

I didn't know what I wanted, but I knew I needed to never see that woman's face staring at the camera and saying, "Please, please." I said to Derek, "Can I have that beer now?"

He gave it to me and smiled. He said, "I'm glad you came out of the bushes, Frank. It was time. Now let's watch the movie."

"I'm going to take a shower." I got up and walked to the bathroom.

"I'm not gonna wait for you to watch it."

"I don't care," I said and shut the bathroom door, took off my clothes, got in the shower. It was too hot, but I didn't have the energy to turn the knobs, making the skin on my chest and stomach turn the color of Pepto-Bismol.

A couple minutes later I heard Derek yell from the other room, "You're a genius!" I couldn't stand anymore and knelt in the tub.

———

I posited earlier that perhaps the only reason people tell stories is to clear their names.

That's certainly why I told you about *The Unveiled Animal* – its unrivaled potential to reshape cinema, its subsequent dormancy, the lowly mishap in the park – hoping you'd see that it truly was my passion, that my intentions were artistic and admirable, that it had been my brother's involvement in it that made the final product so revolting. I'm your Reliable Eyewitness, and I'm also a victim here: Derek had commandeered that which meant the most to me. I couldn't do anything about the gangrenous debacle with the couple now, but what I could do was work on clearing my name via Derek and Mired.

I could tell her the truth, absolve myself from any role in Derek's lie and let all of the responsibility douse him. I'd be doing the right thing, helping Mired, but I'd also be avenging all he'd taken from me that night in the park. It was a kind of vigilante justice, doing the murderous work that went on in the shadows, unsupervised and wild. He'd killed my movie by making me come out of the bushes. Now I could get even.

And as you'll see before the story ends, I accomplished these things and then some: *The Unveiled Animal* reviving, emerging, limbering its muscles, growling, rising up on hind legs, and lunging to kill.

MIRED

Frank and I were still in the kitchen. "What do you mean he dropped me?"

"I don't think it was an accident."

"Why would he hurt me on purpose?"

"He lost his temper."

"But why would he drop me?"

"I came over right after it happened. Derek told me to take you to the hospital because you'd slipped out of his arms while he carried you up the stairs. He was worried you'd think he'd done it intentionally."

"He didn't really open the garage that morning?" I said. The bumblebee still circled the fake rose; the stupid thing couldn't tell the difference between this one and the real thing. Circling it. Landing. Circling. Landing. Mistake after mistake. Idiotic. Doomed. "He just didn't want to come to the hospital?"

"He was worried about himself."

"Can I have some more wine?" I said and finished my whole glass, which was pretty full, before Frank poured the rest of the second bottle into mine. "Why are you telling me now if you've known since the first night?"

"I suspected since the first night. Now hearing that he disappeared this afternoon, I think he's running away."

How long could the bee circle, would it circle? Would it try the same flawed tactics time and again, without learning a thing, until it starved to death in the process?

"So he never actually told you he dropped me," I said.

"I know this is hard for you. But I feel like I need to tell you what I think happened that night. And I think he did it on purpose."

"You don't know for sure."

"I don't know for sure."

"It's time for you to go," I said, and it really was. "I need to lie down."

"No, you don't. You just don't want to listen to me anymore."

"That, too." I couldn't stand it. I stood up and walked over by the bee, waved my hand in the vicinity, and it flew out the window, which I immediately closed to spare the poor thing any further fake-flower humiliation. Then I went to the front door and opened it. I was like a game show host getting rid of a losing contestant. "Good-bye, Frank."

"I'm only trying to help."

"That's not how it feels: you have this look on your face like you're about to cum. Are you enjoying this?"

"Of course not."

"There's euphoria smeared all over your face."

He walked toward me. "This is hard for me, too, Mired."

I tapped my finger on the doorframe. "Derek wouldn't hurt me," I said. "There's no way."

"I know you don't remember, but you said so yourself."

"Said what myself?"

"The night you fell, you asked Derek 'Why did you drop?'"

"I said that?"

"Yeah."

"I don't want to talk to you anymore," I said, circling my own fake flower. Circled and landing, circled and landing. Silly, sad Mired. "He wouldn't hurt me."

Frank walked away, toward the infamous stairs.

"He'd never hurt me on purpose!" I said. "I know that for sure!"

Frank didn't turn around or say anything, disappearing down them, and I yelled, "He'd never do that! There's no way! He loves me!"

DEREK ADMIRES DEAF EARS

It had been four days since she fell, and today, Friday, we had to get out of bed, take showers, plaster happy gags across our faces and venture out into the world, for the first of two trips to the dentist.

I still hadn't found my keys, though I hadn't really tried, hadn't really done much of anything except return the rental car, call in sick for the whole week, and lay around our apartment with Mired.

"How do you know you'll be sick all week?" Nick had said.

"I know myself," I said, which was as big a lie as saying Mired was in good hands.

No keys meant we couldn't drive to the dentist.

"I'll never understand how one man loses his keys so often," Mired said. "You need GPS for everything. What were you doing when you lost them?"

Her question made me remember the way her body got heavier with each step I took, the way it felt as my feet shimmied around on the thin stair, turning around and letting my arms go limp, the way her body flopped, the noises created from bone colliding with concrete, the way I waited until she'd landed at the bottom and ran down and lied to her, and the termites went to work on my heart again, eating it like hunks of watermelon, having to spit out the black seeds, the angry defects that let me do all this in the first place. I thought of our old man, how he'd asked me once when I was a boy, "What if my own heart stopped beating that day in the village? What if it's just the cobra's pounding in my chest and I died years ago?"

We only lived four blocks from the BART station. It was mid-morning, sky clear. The sun was out but a useless prop. This was the first day without fog in a while. Wind shoving freezing air in our faces. We stared at our feet to keep dust and rocks from wedging in our eyes.

Mired walked with a hitch and I asked if her legs hurt, and she said, "Not as much as everything else."

"I'm sorry I can't find my keys."

"Why aren't we in a cab?"

"We both took the week off work. We need to think about money."

"Look at me," she said and pointed at her face. "I don't want to be on the subway looking like this."

We walked by a man muttering to himself, who had his shirt off, a huge tattoo across his chest of an inkblot, one of those Rorschach jobs a shrink shows someone to gauge if they're crazy. My guess is this guy didn't pass the test.

"I can hail a cab," I said to Mired.

"We're almost there."

"I can hail one."

"Forget it."

We went down into the station and bought tickets. The train we needed was boarding as we entered the platform. There weren't very many people on our car. A punk rocker reading Bukowski, huge circular pegs through his earlobes, stretching them the size of a baby's fists. A black man holding a Bible. An older Asian woman carrying plastic grocery bags with stalks of leeks jetting from the tops. A Latino father with his young son sleeping in his lap, stroking his hair. It must have felt nice.

Mired and I boarded the train, sat facing a gay couple, men, about forty. They were probably twenty feet away from us. They were having a vicious argument.

What made their argument so mesmerizing was that they were both deaf, and they argued in sign language. The deaf men yelled with their hands, wrists and fingers conveying gestures of fury, and it looked like the men were the conductors of invisible choirs. Every once in a while one man would mouth a few words at the other, to accent a thought, but mostly they let their hands speak for themselves.

I admired their condition: all they had to do was look away from the other person, and they were saved. Saved from having to hear something they didn't want to.

Mired and I were going three more stops. The train quivered under Market Street, making its way downtown from the Mission district.

"It would have been a ten dollar cab ride," Mired said, yanking a bit on her upper lip, a thing she did when she was nervous or pissed.

"I told you I'd hail one."

"But you didn't."

One of the deaf men punctuated a long series of signs by grunting something that sounded like "Listen," and then crossed his arms and looked away from the other man, looking away and having asylum from his answer.

I bulged with jealousy.

"If you really wanted to hail one," Mired said, "you'd have done it."

I looked away from her, but it did no good, her words still wiggling in my ears.

"I don't think you know how much this hurts," she said.

"I'm sorry."

"Do you think I want people seeing me this way?"

We stopped talking. The train pulled into Civic Center station. No one got on our car.

Once we were moving again, Mired nudged me and pointed at the deaf men, saying, "What do you think's wrong?" Her voice had shed some of its anger.

"How should I know?"

"Let's guess what they're fighting about."

"Why?"

"It'll be fun," she said and smiled, the biggest I'd seen her be able to produce since the accident, showing uneven stumps of teeth.

"I don't want to play."

"I think one's leaving the other," she said.

I stared at her, but I kept thinking about the deaf men's broken ears.

"Play along," she said and yanked on her upper lip again.

"What's the point?"

"Why would one leave the other?"

"No one's leaving," I said. "It's just a fight. They'll work it out."

"I don't think so. This is serious."

She'd started telling me she loved me a lot more since she fell. I don't know why she said it more often, I only know that she did, and I said, "I love you, too." I wasn't sure if I really meant it, but I had to say something, and I wasn't willing to tell her the truth.

Not yet.

I nodded toward the deaf men and asked, "How can you tell it's serious?"

"One's done something unforgivable."

"Like what?"

"I can't tell, but that guy will never love him the way he used to."

"It's just a fight."

"Then what's it about?" she said.

I looked back at the deaf men, but I couldn't bring myself to say anything. I'm sure they had their secrets. Most people do. I'm sure they'd done things they wished to take back or do differently, but life didn't work that way. We acted and there were consequences, assuming your secret got out. I couldn't bring myself to speculate about what the men were arguing about because I admired them too much. They chose what to hear, while the rest of us intercepted all sorts of awful messages we could have lived without.

All I could ask Mired was, "Is this the end?"

"They'll drift apart," she said, tapping her finger on the metallic windowsill, in a rhythm like a heartbeat.

"There's no hope?"

She stopped staring at the deaf men and brought her eyes to mine. One of hers was still swelled closed, still winking. "No. There's no hope."

The train wobbled on in that dark tunnel, buried underneath San Francisco's chaos, all that anger and abuse and violence, all that addiction and numbness. We were buried underneath all the mechanisms that made us struggle on, day after lousy day.

The deaf couple must have reached an understanding because their hands were now still, done talking, just one man resting his head on his lover's shoulder, their body language saying everything.

Neither of us wanted to watch them anymore. Mired looked at her finger, still heartbeat-tapping on the windowsill. I picked up a stray section of the newspaper and read about the *War on Terror*, which was the second to last thing in the world I wanted to be doing. We didn't say anything else until the ride was over. Just sat and breathed – me, Mired, and a million termites. We sat breathing recycled air and the threat of tomorrow.

PART 2
WHAT WENT WORSE

DEREK: STRAIGHT SHINY WHITE TEETH AND BEAUTIFUL PINK LIPS

There was a picture on the waiting room wall. A framed picture of only a mouth. A mouth filled with straight shiny white teeth and beautiful pink lips. The mouth was smiling. I sat there, while the termites plundered my body, cracking bones and gulping marrow and it ran down their tiny feeding-frenzy faces. I was alone and it felt worse than anything, I felt worse than anything, being at the dentist's, knowing what was happening to Mired's mouth, the chiseling and maiming and drilling of her jagged teeth and roots, the mounting of the temporary bridge. Knowing that this was because of me. I knew what she was enduring and I couldn't sit still. Fidgeting. Stomach tied in extraordinary knots, trussed up in ruthless bondage poses. I couldn't stop staring at the mouth filled with straight shiny white teeth and rimmed with beautiful pink lips. It wasn't like I thought the mouth was laughing at me, mocking me. It was just that when I saw the framed perfect smile all I could think about was Mired's smashed one. I knew it was the guilt, the termites, so I said to myself, hey, stay calm, don't panic, just don't look at the framed white teeth and beautiful pink lips, pretend that they're not hanging on the wall, read a magazine or send a text message, do something, anything, to keep your attention from the framed smile. I looked through an issue of *Sports Illustrated*, but even if I liked sports it wouldn't have mattered. All that mattered was the framed smile. I couldn't stop looking at it. I don't care how long it had hung there, or how many people had seen it. The smile was only there to remind me of what I'd done to Mired, the way

I'd lost all control, and I couldn't sit there a second longer, under that billboard of perfect teeth and pink lips, and I popped up, the receptionist looked over at me, smiled, even her teeth were little enamel-guarded opinions, judges and juries disguised as canines and incisors and molars, and these teeth sentenced me to life in prison without parole. I needed to get away from her, too. "Where's the bathroom?" I asked and she pointed to a door and said, "Down the hall, to the right," and I left her smile and the framed smile and locked myself in the lousy bathroom. I took some humungous breaths, washed my hands and face, trying to convince myself that things would work themselves out, but I didn't believe it, and who was left to lie to when you couldn't lie to yourself?

Someone jiggled the handle on the bathroom door. I dried my face and hands, then opened it. Mired stood in front of me, wearing a dental bib with streaks of blood on it.

"Oh, Derek," she said and asked me to hug her and I did.

"Is there anything I can do?"

She shook her head and told me that her mouth really hurt, but when I asked why she didn't request more Novocain, she said she didn't want to because she deserved the pain. She said, "Do you forgive me?"

Termites, like vultures, pillaged the remaining slivers of me. "There's nothing to forgive."

"I hate that I did this to myself," she said, and I said, "Better not keep the dentist waiting too long," and she said, "I love you," and I said, "I love you, too," and she walked into the bathroom and locked the door, and I went to the waiting room and the receptionist smiled at me again and I looked at the straight shiny white teeth and beautiful pink lips and thought about all the blood on Mired's dental bib and her saying, "Do you forgive me?" and that was what I should be asking, and I'd forgotten I'd worn a white shirt and gazed down at it, blots of her blood spotting the shirt, and I made sure not to see the receptionist's smile or the framed one by running out of the office with my head down into the windy day and I took a taxi back to the Mission and tore our apartment apart until I found the keys to my truck buried in the bottom of the laundry hamper.

———

There was nowhere for me to go, no one to talk to, seeing as how I'd left Mired at the dentist's and Frank was acting like some know-it-all detective. And I couldn't talk to Nick. He was at the end of his one-legged rope, sick and tired of all my flakiness. But Nick was the least of my worries, so what if I lost my job? I'd get another one doing the same thing, yanking out the parts that had busted, shoving in new ones to take their place. The only thing I'd miss about working there were the days that Nick wore shorts to the garage and his titanium leg stuck out for everyone to see, looking like the Terminator, if Arnold Schwarzenegger had given up on his mission and let himself go to complete shit.

I punched Reno, Nevada, into my GPS because someone there was bound to be having a worse day than me. Crawled up Highway 80, through Sacramento and the foothills. Hit a snarl of traffic. Over in the fast lane, a guy stood yammering on his cell phone, the hood of his car propped open and smoke drifting out. Another blown gasket. I'll never know why people find it so hard to take care of something as simple as putting water in their radiators. He was wearing a tie and I didn't want to help some swanky white collar working stiff whose asshole smelled like cappuccinos.

———

Three hours later I drove into Reno, its sign welcoming all tourists to *The biggest little city in the world*. A foot or so of snow had fallen recently, not on the road anymore, all shoved to the sides in gray piles that looked like upside-down bathtubs.

I parked my car and walked through the cold, thin air. I smelled cinnamon. I walked to a diner. Runny eggs sounded good. A couple cups of coffee sounded even better. Figuring out what I was supposed to do now sounded the best of all.

The lady waiting on me looked like Mired, an older version of Mired, maybe fifty or so. Her nametag said *Darla*. She took my order and went to get the coffeepot. When she walked over with it and filled my empty cup, she said, "Having a tough go tonight, huh?"

"It's been better."

"Well," she said, "if you haven't been better than eating alone in this crap-factory, I'd be worried about you."

I got the urge to hit on her a little, not that I was interested in sex, just something to make me forget what I was doing here in the first place. I smiled real big. "Thanks for your occupational concern, madam. Are you Filipina?"

"How'd you know that?"

"Shape of the face. Dead giveaway."

"Most of the racists around here think I'm Vietnamese."

I wondered if our old man had ever sat at this very booth, trying to place where he'd seen Darla before. "You don't look Vietnamese at all."

"Hence the word 'racists.'" She coughed. "You having girl trouble?"

"Isn't it always?"

"Not always. But boys and girls do have trouble playing nice together." She shook the coffeepot back and forth. "Just give me a wink when you're ready for a refill."

There was no way to explain that winking was something too hard for me to do.

Once she walked away, I pulled my phone out and called my voicemail. One new message. From Mired. And this was all she had to say to me: *Don't end it this way. I'm sorry. Let's schedule an emergency session with Dr. Montahugh, okay? Don't give up on us now. We're supposed to take care of each other.*

I took a sip of coffee. Too hot. Singed the tip of my tongue.

I erased it, leaned my head back, and lit a cigarette. You've got to love Nevada, a state where you can still smoke anywhere you want. Maybe not anywhere. Probably not preschools or oncology wards, but the point was I could sit in a diner and chain-smoke and no one gave me a second thought.

I took an appreciative drag. Some of the smoke got in my eyes, made me blink like crazy.

Darla walked over and said, "Were you winking at me?" She looked even more like Mired this time. Mired had a cute little upturned nose, and I could tell the waitress used to have one, too, but booze had made its tip swell and look like a baby bootie. "I sure was winking at you."

"Flirt," she said, refilling my coffee. "Mind if I bum a smoke? I just ran out. You can take it out of my tip."

I kept blinking. My eyes watered a little and I ran my finger across them. "Who said I was leaving you a tip?"

"You're bad."

"You can say that again."

"Hold on," she said, frowned and shook the coffeepot. "Got to do the rounds. The whole world is winking at me right now."

I took a cigarette from my pack and handed it to her.

"Thanks, flirt."

"Chivalry is alive and well."

"That may be true," she said, "but it ain't living in Reno."

———

I barely chewed the runny eggs, letting them ooze their way down my throat. The termites went to work inside me again. Not as ravenous as before. These must have been new ones, more sophisticated, nibbling on appetizers while listening to classical music, preparing their posh palettes for the main course.

For the first time, I felt like I should call Frank, should check in with him and see where things stood, not that I really needed an update. I could guess. I assumed Frank had sold me out, and she wanted to hear my side of things, but what was my side?

If I could have told her the truth, I'd have already done it, I'd have spilled the beans during one of the days since I'd dropped her, but every time the words wormed their way to the edge of my tongue, they'd peek over it like a scared child looking down at a pool from the cliff of a high-dive, only to retreat and run down the ladder to safety. The words would chicken out – okay, *I'd* chicken out – and they'd crawl back down into my ransacked guts.

"You finished?" Darla said, wielding the coffeepot again. It always seemed to be full. I appreciated her commitment to keeping her customers caffeinated.

My plate was clean, except for a few streaks of uncooked egg white, a little smudge of ketchup. I took the paper napkin out of my lap, crumpled it, threw it on the plate. "Affirmative, madam. Absolutely delicious."

"Now I know you're full of it."

"Full of what?"

"You and I both know the food here is atrocious."

"If you're hungry enough, the food here's so good it tastes like pussy."

She laughed so hard she snorted. "Anything else I can get you?"

"Just a check."

She pulled it from her apron, set it on the table. "I hope things turn around for you."

"Sooner or later they have to, right?"

"I don't know about that."

"It's the law of averages."

"You think so?" she said.

"I hope so."

"Well, I'm sure as hell still waiting." Then Darla grimaced and looked around the room, using the coffeepot to point at everyone sitting in the diner. "We're all still waiting."

DEREK: GO WOMBATS!

I still wasn't ready to go into a casino, wanting to get a few bourbons in me before I braved the whirling lights and farm boys on crystal meth and people slurping every cent from their welfare checks. Reno didn't get the same stature of customer as Vegas, more hillbillies than celebrities, more bounty hunters than paparazzi. I went into a small bar, played video poker, slugged shots of Wild Turkey. Kept smoking cigarettes. There wasn't a woman in the whole place. Just a bunch of horny lowlifes hunched over electric machines, hoping to make a couple bucks. The guy playing poker next to me clapped his hands and said, "Looks like someone's leaving 49 dollars richer."

I didn't answer him, didn't look at him.

"Don't go thinking you can follow me home, come in my trailer, and steal my loot," he said.

I didn't answer him, watching my machine deal out the next hand of cards, not even a single pair.

"Between you and me no one will ever find where I keep the loot anyway."

I looked over at him: a tiny man, like a horse jockey, hands the size of a nine-year-old girl and wearing yellow puka shells around his neck.

"My cat's been dead for three years," he continued, "but I keep his dirty litter box in the trailer, stuff my loot in the bottom of it. No way will any robber look in there."

Still, I didn't offer a response, sent my eyes back toward my machine. I'd lost again.

"Not a day goes by that I don't miss that little son of a bitch, though."

I put another nickel in, tried to say something nice to the guy, not that I really cared about his dead cat, but I didn't want him busting into tears or anything while I drank bourbon and played poker. "Why don't you get a new one?"

"I miss *my* cat, not some impostor."

"I don't mean an impostor. I mean a new cat that you'll like just as much."

"I'm too loyal for an impostor. He's gone, and he was my first cat, and I owe him the respect of being the only one I ever own. Not that I really owned him. We were friends. Fast friends. Best friends. True friends. When I love someone I'm loyal forever. Even if the new cat looked just like Jarvis, I'd know it wasn't really him."

The machine had dealt me four diamonds, only needed one more for a flush. My cell phone rang again. No need to look and see who was calling. I pushed the button to send her call to voicemail, pushed another button on the machine to get my new card. "Another cat might ease your grief."

"Grief?" he asked me. "Grief? Who said anything about grief? Why would you go bringing up grief?"

I didn't get what I needed for the flush, put in another nickel.

"And forget grief," he said to me. "Maybe this'll be our lucky night, pal. Maybe we'll win the big loot. What would you do first? What's the one thing you've always wanted?"

"A Cadillac. A 1971 Coupe deVille. That baby has a trunk so big I could fill it with whiskey and swim laps. Float on my back and look up at the stars."

His mouth made a smacking noise like he tasted something delicious. "That sounds nice. Where would you go?"

"Nowhere."

"What do you mean?"

"That car gets like four miles to the gallon. I'd be bankrupt before I crossed the state line."

"You're rich, remember? Pretend you just struck the big loot."

"Oh yeah. Forgot. Maybe I'd drive around. Me and my swimming pool out on the highway. Pull over at every rest stop and take a dip." I lost again and put in another nickel and hoped it was only a matter of time before I won something. "You sure you wouldn't want to get a new cat if you hit it big tonight?" I asked him.

"I've hit big lots of times. Problem is I always lose it all the next day."

"Couldn't you buy a cat before you gambled tomorrow?"

"There aren't any 24-hour pet stores in Reno. Besides, no cat could stack up to Jarvis. I'd have to get some other kind of animal. Truth is I've always liked ostriches. Hey, what do you think of ostriches?"

"I know they can run faster than any other bird," I said. Frank had told me that back in high school. "They're the Bugatti Veyron of birds."

"What's that?"

"Bugatti Veyron. Tops out at 253 miles an hour."

"That's one fast ostrich."

"No, it's a sports car."

"I mean, I've never seen a bird haul ass like that."

Lost again and I pumped in more change and sighed. "Only the car can go that fast. But ostriches are damn fast for birds."

"Maybe we'll both get the big loot," Puka Shells said. "We can caravan: you in your Caddy with the built-in swimming pool, and me and my new ostrich cruisin' in a Boogatee Vealron."

"Maybe," I said.

Lousy thing was then he threw up all over his machine. Even

lousier, all he did to clean it up was swipe his teeny hands across the thing, spilling what looked like French dressing all over the floor. He kept on playing, didn't move to a new machine or anything, sat there whispering things about his Jarvis and ostriches and Boogatee Vealrons and pumping in new nickels.

He barely lasted another five minutes, though, because once the bartender got a good whiff and knew someone had tossed his cookies, he walked right over to the culprit. "How many times do we have to talk about this?" the bartender asked him.

"Talk about what?"

The bartender led him to the front door and pushed him outside. A few minutes later, the bartender shuffled over carrying a mop, and I said, "He's done this before?"

"Yup."

"Why do you let him keep coming back?"

"Where else is he going to go? He's been 86'd from every place in town. Plus he's my uncle. Family, you know? Family has to take care of family." He mopped it up and loped back behind the bar.

My cell phone squawked and squawked and squawked. It was always Mired. No one else had called me all day. I half expected Frank to call, issue me another ultimatum, reiterate his plan to never let Mired forgive me.

I'd lost another hand of video poker, going for a full house but coming up short.

The bar's front door opened. A team of men, a literal team, fat guys wearing white sneakers and softball jerseys, waddled in, screaming, "Extra innings victory! You're looking at the first place team in the Nevada indoor softball league! To the victors go the spoils!"

"I don't know about any spoils," the bartender said to the team, "but how about a couple free pitchers of beer?"

Clapping fat hands. White sneakers squeaking on the floor. Men in softball jerseys high-fiving and whooping. Awful moustaches between their noses and mouths, like angry weeds. A couple of them barked like dogs.

The bartender poured three pitchers of beer, pulled chilled plastic mugs from a fridge and filled them. "Congrats on the game, boys."

The whole team held up their draft beers, howling, "Go Wombats!" and adjusting their baseball hats, or were they called softball hats? And how did you play softball indoors? Anyway, hats were adjusted. The light beer was drunk. Suddenly, I wanted to throw up on my video poker machine, too, surrounded by all these Wombats wearing jerseys and ejaculating pride.

I went into the bathroom, which was one of those places that didn't have separate urinals for men to piss in, just a huge trough we all had to belly up to. I pulled my cock out and dialed my voicemail. Two new messages.

The first: *People who love each other are supposed to be there for the bad times.*

Right as I was erasing it, two Wombats wobbled into the bathroom on their squeaky white sneakers. I stood at the middle of the trough, so one of them came up on either side of me.

I was still pissing.

They pulled their pricks from their uniforms.

One of them said, "Never thought we'd beat those surly bastards," and the other said, "We surely did just that," and his buddy said, "We showed those sons of bitches who God is!" and his friend said, "No, we showed them who God *was*. Remember to watch your tenses," and the other one said, "Yeah, yeah, thanks, Professor, we aren't all lucky enough to teach the 7th grade."

While I eavesdropped, I played Mired's next message: *Where did you go? We need to talk. Frank thinks that...*

I erased it before I had to hear the rest.

"What are you doing?" the Wombat situated on my left said.

I tucked the phone between my ear and shoulder. "Who, me?"

"Yeah, you. Who else might I be directing my question to?"

The other Wombat leaned forward, toward the trough, so he could see us as we spoke.

"What's wrong?" I said, letting my dick hang free and shutting the phone, which I stuffed in my pocket.

"I believe you peripherally relieved yourself on my shoe," he said.

"He do what now, Professor?" his friend said.

"No, no, he's already done it," Professor said. "You meant to say, 'He's done what now?'"

"I meant what?" his friend said.

"I didn't piss on anyone's shoe," I said.

"You most certainly did. Look," and he pointed to his right shoe, right next to me. It didn't look wet. He said, "You were talking on your phone and you leaned back a little and urine splashed all over my shoe."

"On whom's shoe had he pissed?" his friend said.

"Both of you be quiet and let me think," Professor said.

"I didn't piss on your shoe," I said, shaking the last couple drips and tucking it away. "Maybe he did it," and I motioned to the other guy.

"Bruce?" Professor said.

"I don't know his name."

"How could he urinate on my shoe from all the way over there?"

"Superior aim?"

"Listen," Professor said, "that gentleman standing next to you is my centerfielder, Bruce. We carpool to work together. We're neighbors. Why would he urinate on my shoe?"

"I'm not saying he pissed on your shoe," I said. "I'm just saying I didn't."

"Actually, you are saying he pissed, to use your harsh parlance, on my shoe. Because if you're saying you didn't, there's no one else here except good old Bruce."

"Yeah, no one but Bruce," Bruce said.

"If I did, it was an accident," I said, walking over to wash my hands.

"There's no if, sir. You did it, unequivocally."

"Sorry," I said.

"You don't sound sorry."

The Wombats had finished pissing and stood behind me.

"You sound unsorry," Bruce said.

"Shut up," I said.

"You want Bruce to shut up?" Bruce said.

"Stay calm, gentlemen," Professor said. Then to Bruce: "There's no such word as 'unsorry.'" Then to me: "Despite his diction, Bruce brings up a valid point. You don't sound sorry. You sound like you're only extending contrition to get out of this mess you've made. You sound like you think this is funny. So do you? Do you think this is funny?"

I dried my hands and threw the towel toward the trash can. Missed. I turned to leave. "Good evening to you, gents."

The two Wombats stood in my way.

"Answer me, please," Professor said. "Is this funny?"

Bruce stuck his fingers out, weakly pushing me, pushing me like he knew he had a slew of softball backup, but otherwise, if it was the two of us, he knew I'd kick his ass all over the bathroom.

"You got something to say to Bruce?" Bruce said.

And then I grabbed him. Lousy thing was I knew I was outnumbered no matter what, so I figured I'd go for an early knockout, take care of these two without the other Wombats knowing about it and get out of the bar as fast as I could. I hoped to overwhelm Bruce with my wily strength and he'd surrender and then I could take care of the Professor, but Bruce wrestled back, I got my arms around him good, got them like this: one between his legs, one under an armpit, and I picked him up, pausing once he was in my arms, pausing and thinking of the night

I'd dropped Mired down the stairs, and as I held him, thinking of her, the Professor cold-cocked me right in the kidney. I fell over backward, and Bruce crash-landed on top of me.

Professor ran to the door and said, "We need every Wombat in the place to come here now! It's a team emergency!" and I heard the stampede of squeaking softball sneakers, and there I was, on the floor, underneath Bruce, a Wombat, completely outnumbered.

They barreled into the bathroom.

Professor pointed at me and said, "This gentleman has wronged not one, but two Wombats. First, he micturated on my shoe. Then…"

"He 'mic-tuh-whatted'?" some Wombats asked.

"Micturated. Urinated. Pissed. This bozo whizzed on my shoe! Then he challenged ol' Bruce to a fight!"

One man stepped forward. Maybe their manager. Their best player. I don't know, but he was definitely in charge. "Okay, there are two outs," he said. "It's the bottom of the ninth. What are we going to do?"

"WE'RE GOING TO PLAY BALL!" they all said.

"I CAN'T HEAR YOU, WOMBATS!"

"WE'RE GOING TO PLAY BALL!"

"WHAT?"

"PLAY BALL!"

"THEN LET'S PLAY BALL WITH THIS SORRY SON OF A BITCH, WOMBATS!" he said.

Bruce wiggled off of me, and the Wombats leaned down and picked me up. They all pitched in, hoisting me in the air. Soon I was as high as they could lift me, like I was on their team and had done something amazing, won a game in the final inning and salvaged a victory that seemed out of reach but we'd pulled it out in the end, and now they held me up in celebration. They celebrated me. My contribution. They cherished what I'd done because what I'd done was spectacular. I hadn't hurt anyone, hadn't lied about it, hadn't run away to Reno, or dodged phone calls, hadn't hated myself more than any other time in my whole life or felt the lousy termites ravage my organs. I was just another Wombat enjoying a beer from a free pitcher, squeaking my white sneakers and fluffing my moustache. I was on the team and I'd done something wonderful and here we were, a bunch of ecstatic Wombats tearing up the town.

But that wasn't why they held me up in the air. That wasn't what they had in mind at all. Because then the Wombats dropped me into the trough. I landed on my back and kept my eyes closed and the urinal cakes jammed against my spine. I lay in there for ten or fifteen seconds before their salty softball trickles trickled all over me. I didn't even fight or squirm, no reason to, just lay back and tried to cover my mouth with my hands as they baptized me. I lay back and tried not to breathe and let every memory of what I'd done to Mired pelt me along with their streams, and I imagined the trough filling up entirely with Wombat piss and the bathroom filling too and then Reno and San Francisco and every other sad American town and then the whole world would disappear under an ocean of urine and we'd all struggle and we'd all drown and I felt a type of lousiness I'd never known before.

DEREK: BE BETTER

The only game I remember our old man playing with us was when he'd throw me on the ground and sit on my chest and grab me by the wrists and use my hands to hit my own face, and he'd say, "Why are you hitting yourself, Derek? Why are you hitting yourself?" and I'd laugh and try to fight him off, try to fight me off, try to make my hands not hit my face, but I couldn't keep my hands from hitting my face, and he'd be winking at me every once in a while, saying, "Why do you keep hitting yourself?" and the longer he sat on me the harder he made my hands hit my face, and by the tenth time he rammed my hand into my face with so much force my cheek would burn and he'd be winking and Frank would be standing right around us, saying, "It's my turn," and my dad would say, "Derek won't stop hitting himself, Frankie," and Frank would say, "Make me hit myself. It's my turn," and our dad would hold one of my hands inches from my face and he'd make it shake a little, pretending like he was trying to stop me from hitting myself, and he'd say to Frank, "I don't think I can hold it back for much longer!" still shaking my arm, and Frank would laugh and my dad would laugh and I'd get one last wink from the old man before my hand hit my face again, the old man rolling off of me and pinning Frank to the floor.

———

I'm not sure why I wanted to tell you about our old man saying, "Why do you keep hitting yourself?" The point could be that he made it all the way back to the States before going MIA, doing us a favor, maybe, leaving our village before the massacre. Or the point could be my mom doesn't want to talk to me, must have seen bits of our old man in my nature and she hadn't been a mother to me in a long time. Or Frank conspiring against me. But really, the point was that I crawled out of a pissing trough in a men's room in Reno, Nevada, soaked in softball-trickles, pushing the bathroom door open and walking by the Wombats, who laughed and hollered under their moustaches, squeaking their sneakers, howling between slurps of light beer, and I had to hear one of them say, "What's that smell?" while waving his hand in front of his face just like I'd done to Mired and her chicken parmesan, the guy pointing at me, and another Wombat said, "Smells like a urinal," and another said, "Where's it coming from?" and another said, "I don't know," and another said, "I think it's coming from him," and another came over close to me and sniffed me and said, "Oh, yeah, here's the problem," and Professor said, "You better vacate the premises. Wombats are a temperamental species," and another said, "We'll give you ten seconds before we do it again. Guzzle your beers to reload, Wombats!" and I was almost to the front door, and they guzzled their beers, and one finished his and said, "Go, Wombats!" and Bruce said, "Go Wombats!" and then I was outside, snow falling for the first time since I'd been in Reno, ran to my truck, revved the engine and cranked the heater up all the way.

———

Eventually, I took some clean clothes out of my duffel bag and changed. Not right away, though. First I sat in my truck. Mad and scared. If I still owned a gun, I'd have gone right back into the bar and hunted some Wombats. But I didn't own a gun, hadn't had one in years, since two-faced Frank stole mine, though he'd deny it to this day. He stole it after we pretended to rob a couple and filmed the whole thing. My brother, all bark but didn't have a tooth in his mouth to bite with. He'd been going on and on about becoming a filmmaker ever since high school, about changing the whole film business with his *Unveiled Animal*, and we finally got some good footage, but Frank backed down, chickened out, which was why it was so strange that he stood up to me over this thing with Mired: for years he'd bark, bark, bark, but he never showed a tooth that could puncture my thick skin.

Last thing I did after taking off my soaked clothes and pitching them out the window onto the snow was light another cigarette. Smoking and thinking. Fighting back crying, all those bastards pissing all over me, and I kept telling myself to stop being such a pansy, to stop crying, what would the old man say? He'd feel his cobra's heartbeat and go right back in the bar, armed, unarmed, he wouldn't care, he'd go back in there and shush every Wombat, take on every one of them that came his way. Win or lose, he wouldn't care, that wouldn't be the point, the point would be dignity, manhood. The point would be kill or be killed. The point was while these guys played softball, our father fought the memories of My Lai, and you'd have to break his arms and legs before he'd stop coming after you. He never sat in a truck crying in his entire life. And if he had, it wasn't because of what other people had done to him. It was because of what he'd done. He never threw piss-soaked clothes out of his truck window and drove off with a wet tail wedged between his legs.

I punched the GPS off the dashboard, stomped on it once it hit the floor. Then killed time, driving around Reno. A little drunk from the Wild Turkey. Driving up and down the same streets. Busted GPS and no sense of direction. The winking lights from the casinos seemed like the saddest things in the entire world. Lousy lights inviting working stiffs to come inside and ruin their lives. Ruin them more. Pitch their lives in the trough and drown them. Let all the failures fill their lungs. Drowning in their failures so the aching would stop. And my hair was still wet from all the Wombat piss. And every one of Mired's messages seemed to replay itself in my head. At the same time. They talked over one another. All the words piling on in loud, mad voices. It was like surveillance bugs, tiny devices used to steal conversations from strangers, it was like I had all these surveillance bugs in my head broadcasting Mired's angry and wicked and miserable and devastated voices at the same time, and I had nowhere to go, couldn't drive all the way to Cleveland, couldn't go home, couldn't go to my mom's house, not after all this time. She hadn't called or written or emailed since the last time I let her down, skipping my grandfather's funeral. She'd given up. She was tired of me. Everyone was tired of me, except Mired, and now I'd ruined that, too. Leaving her at the dentist's. Walking out while she had her teeth drilled to bits. How did I do that?

She's in good hands.

I had no home left. No mom or Mired or Frank. No one would have me. I was alone and stuck knowing what I'd done to Mired, stuck with the starving termites as tenants, wandering Reno, one of the most abysmal places ever, and I thought of that bartender saying, "Family has to take care of family," after his uncle had thrown up on the video poker machine, but the bartender was wrong. Family didn't have to take care of family, but it must be nice when it worked out that way.

I kept driving in pointless circles, my window cracked so the smoke could escape, but then I rolled it up, wanting the cigarette reek to drench my clothes, my skin, my wet hair, wanting the smell of smoke to cover up every trace of what the Wombats had done.

———

Nowhere to go, and I ended up back at the diner. Figured I could flirt with the old waitress a little more. Lousy thing was that had been the highlight of my night. If I couldn't be around my Mired, the aged one would have to do.

It was only 6 p.m. The diner didn't have the same bustle as before. She greeted me with a huge, exaggerated wave as I walked in. "Back for more eggs that taste like pussy?" she said.

"Better than that coffee of yours. Shit tastes like hydrogen peroxide."

"Amen to that. You all right? You don't look so good."

"I'll pull through. I came to see you, Darla."

"That's right. Mr. Flirt. How could I forget? So I'm assuming you don't want any more coffee?"

"I'm going to pass on that, thanks. They say the definition of insanity is doing the same thing over and over and expecting different results."

"Who says that?"

"Lots of people."

"That's one of the problems, I guess," Darla said. "People love to make things more complicated than they really are. The definition of insanity is being fucking crazy."

"Can I have a beer, please?"

She listed the choices. I said Bud was fine. She brought me the beer bottle and said, "Do you want a glass?"

"It's already in a glass."

She shook her head. "You've got a line for everything, huh?"

"Still trying to find a good one for global warming."

"What really brings you back?"

"I came to say hi."

"Oh, did you?" she said. "Bad news, I'm spoken for. Married sixteen blasé years."

"Blasé? That doesn't sound very good."

"It's better than hostile. Or violent. Adulterous or alcoholic or absentee. At least he doesn't spike drugs or look at kiddie-porn."

"When you put it like that 'blasé' sounds great."

I opened up my cigarettes, lit two, handed her one. She took a drag and blew smoke out of her nose and said, "I never thought I'd say this, but blasé is just about as much as anyone can hope for, I think."

"I could use some advice. Can you sit down for a minute?"

She and I looked over at her other tables. Four, total. Everyone was eating. One guy waved an empty syrup container at her. She sighed. "Let me go make sure none of the babies need anything. Then you'll have my undivided attention."

Once she walked away, I could hear a radio coming from the kitchen, playing "You Can't Always Get What You Want."

She checked on all of them. I could hear her bickering with one of the tables. Some guy wanted to send back his tuna melt for being too fishy.

"Are you joking?" she said.

"It tastes too much like fish."

"It is fish."

"Yeah, but this is really, really fishy."

"Sorry, sugar. No refunds. Maybe you'll have better luck at the casinos."

"I like your bad attitude," the guy said to her. "Can I take you out some time?"

She shut her eyes, puckered at him, made a smooching noise. "Not even the tide would take you out, honey."

As she walked away, the guy with the tuna melt scowled, though the other men at his table laughed. She slid into the booth across from me and said, "Now what's got you feeling so doom's day?"

"Another smoke?"

"My, my, you are fanatical concerning your nicotine intake."

I lit two again and handed her one.

"It's my girlfriend. She had an accident."

"What kind of accident?"

"Well, we were… drunk. Very drunk. Driving home from a party and she passed out in the car. I tried to carry her up our stairs, and she wiggled from my arms and fell down them."

"Is she all right?"

I nodded. I nodded a lot. I took a drag and nodded some more. "Oh, yeah." More nodding. "But she knocked her teeth out. Broke her wrist. Some bruises and cuts."

"That's horrible."

"It is."

"But you didn't tell me what's actually wrong."

"She thinks I did it on purpose."

"Did what?"

"Dropped her."

"Why does she think that?"

"I don't know," I said. "She told me she didn't remember much from that night, but that she remembers me turning around and dropping her down the stairs."

"But you didn't."

"I love her."

She scoffed. "My ex-husband Daryl loved me. I really believe that. But he still put a bar of soap in a sock and came swinging it at my head when he thought I was running around on him."

"I'm glad he didn't hit you with it."

"Who said he didn't hit me with it?"

I stubbed out my cigarette, finished my beer. She asked if I wanted another bottle, but I told her no, not yet.

"Were you running around on him?" I said.

"Did you drop her on purpose?"

"No."

"Then I wasn't running around on him." She winked at me. "But I hope you didn't. You're a young man. You can still decide the kind of person you want to turn into. And don't decide to be another wife-beating asshole. The world's got plenty of those. Plenty of Daryls. You work on being a good one."

"I'll take that beer now."

She winked again. "I'll be right back," and barely thirty seconds later, she slid into the booth, not even enough time for the termites' teeth after I'd lied to her. "It's already in a glass, right?" she said.

"Exactly."

"What are you going to do?"

"About Mired?"

"If that's her name, yes."

"I don't know."

"Did she press charges?"

"No. She's, I think, still sorting through the story."

"Sounds like she has her doubts about you."

"I guess."

She put her hand out across the table and touched mine: "The important thing is that you didn't do it."

"Right."

"If you two really love each other, you'll work this out. Otherwise, you won't. I've done enough living to know that life goes on, even when you can't imagine how."

This made me think of our dad. I'd have heard, probably, if he was dead. So where was he? Had he found a way to slaughter his squealing demons? Or was he somewhere tussling with the memories of everyone he murdered that day? Or was it just him and the cobra's heartbeat, the only thing left he could hear?

There was something in the moment that let me do it, let me tell Darla the truth. It might have been how much she looked like an older version of Mired or maybe the Wombats or my disappeared dad. I don't know. But Darla and I were two working stiffs sitting in a diner, and Daryl had hit her with a sock full of bar soap, and I leveled with her: "I dropped Mired on purpose."

"I already knew that."

"How?"

"I'm a poker player, and you're a bad liar. I wouldn't play any cards on my way out of town, if I was you."

"I'm sorry," I said. No termites. Just me sitting there telling the truth.

"Don't apologize to me. She's the one that has to forgive you."

"Do you think she will?"

"I don't know. But I sure as hell wouldn't."

I finished my beer. "What do I owe you for these?" I said and shook the empty bottle.

"They're on the house."

I stood up to leave. "Can I hug you?"

She smiled and said, "Of course you can." We hugged and Darla didn't say anything about the way I smelled, the way the Wombats had left me. "Are you going to tell her the truth?"

"I can't."

"You can."

"I don't think so."

"It won't be easy, but you can do it."

We were still hugging. "How?"

And really, how? How do you do that? It seemed like such a simple question but was lousy with possibilities, all the ways it could ruin your life. How do you tell the truth when it might mean losing everything? Where's the courage for honesty if it can confiscate everything you have?

Did our old man tell people the truth? *Were you in Vietnam?* Yeah, I was in Vietnam. *Did you see active combat?* I saw active combat. *Did you kill anyone?* Yeah, I killed some folks. *Were they all soldiers?* No. *Who were they?* We stormed My Lai and murdered a few hundred Vietnamese civilians. *Why did you do it?* I was told to. *But why did you do it?* It was a war. *That's not a reason.* Does there have to be a reason? *Yes, of course, there has to be a reason. Why did you do it?* I don't know. *Why did you do it?* I don't know. *Why not?* I'm not sure. *Why?*

Maybe we were always asking ourselves that question in our own ways: why?

Darla pulled her head back so we were close, looking right into each other's eyes. It was like staring into the future, a crystal ball. It was like time travel, staring at my life, at what my life would be, if I ever told Mired the truth and she forgave me. And even if she was able to, how would I forgive myself?

"Be better than Daryl," Darla said.

———

Out front of the diner, sitting in my truck, feet planted next to the busted GPS. It was still snowing. I thought about calling our mom and telling her about my My Lai. Thought maybe she'd know what to do, how to do it, because she'd listened to our old man moan for all those years. But I couldn't call her. It would be rotten having to tell her that I'd turned into our old man and that I was another violent and sick and selfish human. I was captain of the lousy-scale. I couldn't blame him. I couldn't try and excuse dropping Mired because of what he'd done. Life wasn't that easy. It was me. I was me. I was responsible. And the secret I carried was a thousand pounds and infected and righteous with hate. It wasn't my mom I needed to call. Maybe someday we'd salvage things, who knows? Right then I needed to talk to Mired. I couldn't put it off any longer. Part of me hoped she'd have her earplugs in, that she'd have no way of knowing I was calling, confessing to prove I wasn't another Daryl, but she picked up after the third ring.

"Where are you?" she said.

"Driving around."

"Come home."

"I can't."

"I need you to."

I stomped on the GPS as hard as I could. "I'm sorry I left you at the dentist."

"I thought you broke up with me."

"No," I said and was fighting back tears, the termites rubbing wasabi on the backs of my eyes, getting them nice and spicy before they dug in for another course. "I was carrying you up the stairs when you fell. You wiggled out of my arms."

"Why didn't you tell me that in the first place?"

"Because I feel awful."

"It was an accident."

"But I hurt you," sobbing now, stomping the GPS again, plastic splintering.

"Come home, Derek."

"You wiggled…"

"I need you. Right now. Come home."

"I can't."

"Why not?"

"I hurt you," and my eyes burned so badly that I couldn't keep them open, squeezing them shut as hard as I could, tears still leaking from the faulty seals. I punched the steering wheel.

"Please," she said.

"You wiggled."

"Frank thinks you…"

"It wasn't my fault."

"Where are you?" she said.

"In my truck."

"Come home."

"I'm so sorry I hurt you," I said and punched the steering wheel again, kicked the wrecked GPS one last time and how would I find my way now?

I was whimpering and lousy and I dropped Mired again, the phone falling to the truck's floor. Even though it was down at my feet, its volume was loud enough that I heard her say, "Will you please come home?"

I thought about the arguing deaf men we'd watched on that BART train, how I'd envied their ability to look away from the other's furious hands and be safe from things they didn't want to hear. But that wasn't what I wanted anymore. I didn't have to be another Daryl.

"Will you come home?" Mired said, the phone still laying by my feet. Her voice sounded faint and raspy, like an astronaut's calling earth, or a soldier's crackling over an old radio line. I heard everything Mired said, but there was no way I could reach for her.

MIRED: PLASTIC FLOWERS AND FAKE TEETH

Exhibit X? Y? Z? What came after Z?

There needed to be more than twenty-six letters in the alphabet to catalogue my litany of consolations. I needed a more complex alphabet. Hundreds of letters, letters like stars marking selfish constellations. Apparently, I had a fresh one to add to the list, and his name was Derek. Derek, my current catastrophe. His face needed to be chiseled into my Mt. Rushmore of Male Failures, those glib carvings, cemented sneers, all of the men and the ways they had taken advantage of me, hurt me, underestimated me, hated me, omitted the truth, twisted the truth to acquit themselves from wrongdoings, perjured themselves, hit me, raped me, the ones who told me what I wanted to hear, told me sadistic things no one should hear, pretended to be happy, pretended to be unhappy, pretended to be ambivalent, pretended to leave town, never called me after sex, never opened their eyes during sex, scowled at me during sex, never kissed me afterward, never collapsed into my arms afterward but fled to the shower, fled to their clothes and then to obligations outside front doors, the ones who dribbled emotional propaganda to get me into bed faster, so they could cum faster, so they could go home faster or send me home faster, not even offering cab fare, the ones who never tried to make me orgasm, the ones who couldn't make me orgasm, the few that could but lost interest in putting in the effort, the one who wouldn't drive me to the abortion clinic, the one who stole my Charlie Parker CDs, the one who dropped my toothbrush in the toilet and left it there, the one who threw a drink on a homeless man right in front of me, the one who swiped my favorite Hawaiian shirt, the one who crashed my car on a race to the liquor store before last call and didn't tell me he'd dented it. The one who told me the earrings by his bed belonged to his male roommate, his male roommate who the following morning I noted *did not have his ears pierced*. The one who threw up all over the dirty dishes in my kitchen sink and didn't clean it up. The one who told me I'd have to sleep on his couch after we'd screwed because his dogs got upset if strangers slept in bed with them. The one who put a cigarette out on the cover of *The Bell Jar*, a book that had traveled with me since high school. The one who liked to pick me up from the side of the road like I was a hitchhiker and drove to remote streets and wanted me to fight him off during sex. The one with the tiniest penis I'd ever seen who wanted me to tell him how deep he went into me. The one who lost his temper and punched a picture of Frida Kahlo on my wall, leaving his bloodied fist-smudge across her face, saying, "I wish I could hit you instead." The one who didn't say, "I wish I could hit you instead," and just did it. The one who smashed a plant in my kitchen and stormed out, and I couldn't bring myself to clean it up, leaving it there in a heap, leaves going from green to brown to black, as I stepped over pieces of shattered terra cotta for weeks, and my current catastrophe, Derek, the son of a bitch, who threw me down the stairs and had been lying to me ever since he'd done it.

I knew his story was a lie, as soon as he changed the slightest detail. That was who Derek was, someone who'd do anything to avoid consequences. I'd been navigating this trait of his the whole time we dated, but never anything this serious. Usually lies about banal things – why he wasn't coming home that night, where the majority of his paycheck disappeared to, who he was spending time with after work, always saying, "I'm out with the guys," and I'd ask, "What guys?" and he'd say, "No one you know," and I'd say, "Can I come meet you and the guys for a drink?" and he'd say, "Mired, I'm not doing anything wrong."

I'm not doing anything wrong.

His mantra. The chorus to his favorite song. The song he always sang, silently sang, emitting it from secret voices that lived inside him as he walked through his life trying to avoid punishments for his selfish behavior.

I'm not doing anything wrong. If you have to say it…

He kept saying that I'd *wiggled* out of his arms. And *wiggled* was what confirmed the doubts in my mind that Frank had manufactured. How naïve did Derek think I was? Was I supposed to swallow that I was so drunk I couldn't walk up the stairs, so drunk he had to carry me, but that I then had the strength to *wiggle* out of his arms? And why would I want to get out of his arms, if I was that drunk and vulnerable? Derek was a pretty strong guy, and suddenly he couldn't keep me from wiggling too much?

No way.

He was lying, and I finally knew it. Have you ever had a moment like that, a moment in your life when you knew, you really knew that something you'd cherished had turned rancid? He used the word *wiggle*, and there were no more trimmings of uncertainty: he'd dropped me on purpose. He'd taken my teeth. My teeth! He'd broken my wrist. My wrist! He'd cut up my face, mashed my eye shut. And he'd taken something much worse: the truth. He'd made me think I'd done this to myself; he'd confiscated the facts. He'd looked me right in the eyes and lied. I knew Derek wasn't perfect. Of course I knew that. But I thought we were trying to become better people together, which was why we went to Dr. Montahugh. I thought that for the first time in our lives, we were trying to burn all our tawdry motives and gaudy aspirations so they'd vanish, so we could be good to each other.

Because he could be really good to me. He had been, for a

lot of our relationship. Derek never expected me to persevere, to pretend that life wasn't cloying, the way my mom did. Derek didn't want me to JUST go on. He wanted me to feel the way I wanted to feel that day, any day, no matter how pall or pitiful or lonely. No matter the Dostoyevsky/ Plath/ Eeyore factor.

I'd say, "I'm depressed today."

He'd say, "The doctor is prescribing another cocktail."

Or I'd say, "Things seem impossible right now. Just breathing is like running a marathon."

He'd say, "Impossible? Who said the odds were as good as impossible?"

———

It wasn't only men who failed in my relationships. I'd failed, too, and the most painful was Robert. I'd met him in the grocery store. Or maybe it's more accurate to say that he'd met me there. I was standing in front of the variety of bagged lettuces. They didn't have the spinach I normally purchased, so I was comparing prices between the remaining two brands. I put the cheaper of them in my basket.

"I knew it," this man, Robert, said, suddenly standing right next to me.

"Excuse me?"

"I knew you'd choose that spinach." I walked away, but he trailed behind me, still talking, "Don't you want to know how I knew?"

"No thanks," I said, rudely, trying to help this dense member of the opposite herd accept the fact that I wasn't going to have sex with him over a bag of spinach.

"I noticed it when you picked up shaving cream," he said. "I noticed because I was standing next to you grabbing the same kind. Then I looked in your basket and noticed that we had exactly the same items. And since then, I've followed you around the store, and I have to tell you, we've bought exactly the same things. Isn't that a coincidence?"

I stopped walking. I was standing next to a bunch of cans of black beans. "Were you going to buy any beans?" I asked.

"No."

I threw a can in my basket, smirked, said, "Sorry to burst your bubble," and walked away again.

Still, he followed: "You don't want those beans. You're only doing that to get rid of this outrageous man who's following you around the grocery store. Listen, I'd do the same thing. I totally understand! But look at what we've got here." He rifled through the items in his basket: "Salami, hummus, English muffins, sharp white cheddar cheese, broccoli, two bottles of the same red wine, shaving cream, spinach."

"Don't forget about my beans," I said.

"Should I go grab a can?"

"I don't care what you do."

"You have to admit," he said, "it's an odd coincidence."

I stopped walking again, turned to look at him. He had the oddest eyes I'd ever seen; they jetted out from the sockets like the tips of hardboiled eggs.

"But what if it isn't a coincidence at all?" I said. "What if you've skulked behind me the whole time and picked out all the same things, so you could then come up and say what an unbelievable coincidence it was, in the hopes that I'd take you home and screw your brains out?" I started walking again.

"No, no. Please," following behind. "I don't want to give you the wrong idea. I'm not some creep. I'm no deviant. I'm just a guy who was shopping and noticed you had the exact same things as me. I'm sorry if I offended you. I'll leave you alone. Have a nice day."

He turned and walked in the opposite direction.

I don't know why, but I called after him, "What's next?"

He stared at me.

"If we're buying all the same stuff," I said, "what was going to be the next thing I bought?"

"Chicken."

"Legs or breasts?"

"Breasts."

I smiled at him. "Are you some sort of poultry psychic?"

"Nope. But that's what I'm going to get next, too."

His eyes, those jetting egg-eyes were beautiful. Even if he was lying, and at the time, I assumed he was, he got credit for creative pick-up tactics. He tried harder than most men and their wilting one-liners. And besides, I was going to buy three more things after the chicken, and I wanted to see if he was telling the truth, if he knew everything I was going to get. I said, "You're walking the wrong way if you need poultry."

He dashed back to me and said, "I'm Robert."

"Come on, clairvoyant-chicken-man," I said. "Let's go shopping."

———

Robert had been completely correct about the rest of my groceries, our groceries. After chicken breasts, we bought eggs, tamari almonds, whiskey. We checked out one after the other in line, and the girl behind the counter looked at us like we were crazy.

"Is this a joke?" she said.

"Ask him," I said.

———

Robert and I had left the store and were having a couple beers in a neighborhood bar. We were playing nice, enjoying our small talk, until I told him I was going to go out front to smoke a cigarette.

"Those things will kill you," he said.

"Everything kills you."

"That's not true."

"Even the sun gives you cancer. How screwed up is that?"

"Everything in moderation," he said and smiled at me.

"I don't believe it matters."

"Don't believe what matters?"

"The kind of life we lead. It's all chance. Some people die young and some don't. It has nothing to do with being a good or bad person."

Robert agreed that chance played a role in our lives, but he didn't think it was the only factor. He explained his belief in a pluralist fate, that people had many fates laid out before them like hundreds of fingers on a huge hand and through the course of our actions, the way we defined ourselves through deeds done and undone, our fates were narrowed down to a particular direction and finally pinpointed.

"What does that have to do with chance?" I said.

He took a sip from his beer. He was the first man I'd ever hung around who drank light beer. "We should try to lead lives that impact others in a positive way."

"I don't understand how it matters."

"Why not?"

"Sometimes when I'm missing my dad, I look up the ages of horrid people to see how long they lived. I don't know why I do it. Sounds weird, but it soothes me to see the appalling randomness of life, chance burning all around us like wicks. That it wasn't something personal against him. Did you know Stalin was seventy-four when he died? Mobutu was sixty-six and lived with prostate cancer for thirty years. Charles Manson is still alive, in his seventies. And my dad barely made it to fifty. Explain that."

"I'm sorry about your father," he said.

"Brain cancer."

"How old were you?"

"Seven."

"Is your mother alive?"

"In her own way," I said

"They're anomalies."

"Who are?"

"Stalin and Manson. I don't know who the other guy is you

mentioned. They are anomalies. I'm very sorry to hear about your father. He shouldn't have died so young."

"Shouldn't have?"

"I'm sure the world was better while he was a part of it."

My beer was empty; his still had two-thirds left.

"This is boring," I said.

"What's the harm in believing?" he asked. "How can believing hurt you? You're going to live out your days regardless of how many you actually have left, so why not live them in a way you can be proud of?"

"Because you're describing a pacifier. A security blanket. I don't need it. I need the truth, and the truth is there are no rewards for good lives lived and no punishments for our atrocities. We breathe; we get tumors; we die."

He shook his head. "Why even get out of bed if that's the way you think?"

"Bed sores," I said.

———

Yes, my mom was alive and healthy and living in New York, but we weren't close. We'd never been close; when I was young, she kept herself incredibly busy, and she dated a lot, which meant I spent a lot of time alone during junior high and high school. That isn't meant to be a criticism, more an observation. Okay, maybe bringing it up is a way of criticizing. I wondered why she didn't wait until I was out of the house to troll for another husband. If I was sixteen and moving out of the house in two years, why not spend time with me, actually get to know me? Why not make sure your daughter had the skills to leave the nest and be a healthy, self-sufficient woman? But she didn't seem too interested in any of that.

And now, she had difficulty interrupting the rhythm of her life to talk to me, incorporating her patronizing speeches into her daily routines. Whenever I talked to her I could hear her doing other things in the background. Washing dishes. Drawers opening and closing. The toilet flushing. Chewing her cereal, the only thing she'd let herself eat, always starving herself to stay fit, cereal she'd poured and then forgotten about, so when she finally ate it, the flakes were mush, making noises like a wet mop slobbering on linoleum.

She'd put me on speakerphone and straighten her hair.

Speakerphone so she could apply a glycerin facial mask.

Speakerphone to write checks.

To clasp a sports bra and change her outfit eight times before going to the gym, saying, "Uh-huh, uh-huh," in a way I knew meant she wasn't listening at all, but looking at herself in the mirror.

I remember once while I was telling her about the guy with dreadlocks who'd shaved my head, she interrupted me by saying, "Oh, crap."

"What?" I said.

"Crap. Crap." I heard her throw something down.

"What?"

"My toes closed," she said.

"Huh?"

"I'm painting my nails, and I closed my toes, and now they're ruined. I wanted to wear open-toe sandals, and I'm already late for my appointment."

"Mom," I said, "he shaved my head."

"I'll have to wear the brown boots," she said.

———

Robert and I had our first official date three days later. He took me to an upscale raw food restaurant. He was a vegan. We ordered an organic wine, which was so awful I wondered if pesticides made things taste good.

"I have to ask you something," I said. "Not to beat a dead horse, but had you seen me in that grocery store before? Is that how you knew what I'd buy?"

"I hadn't seen you before."

"Why were you buying cheese, salami, chicken, and eggs, if you're a vegan?"

"For my roommate."

"It's just so unbelievable."

"Of course it is," he said. "You don't believe in anything, remember?"

"That's not true."

"Name one thing."

I held up a bite of lukewarm parsnip puree wedged on a leaf of endive. "I believe I like my food hotter than this."

He frowned.

"I'm sorry," I said, "but it's too much for me." I was still holding up the bite of tepid food. "Are you using these vegetables to brainwash me into believing?"

"Of course I am."

"Seriously?"

"Once you take that bite," he said, "there's no turning back."

We were laughing. He blinked a lot when he laughed, his eyelids stretching out like fish mouths breathing to cover up his jetting eyes.

I held the bite of food up in the air like it was a shot of booze and I was making a toast. I said, "Here's to believing." I put it in my mouth and chewed. It tasted terrible. I washed it down with a sip of organic wine, which made me grimace even more.

———

After dinner, he drove me home and I invited him into my apartment. "What would you like to drink?" I said. "I've got whiskey. And vodka. Some Pinot noir." I reached into the back depths of my dirty refrigerator, its light bulb burned out for months. I grabbed a small bottle buried way in there and pulled it to the front so I could see what it was. "And one old beer."

"Mmmm. Stale ale."

He kissed me while my hand held the old beer.

———

We had sex. Odd sex. It wasn't bad, but I can't say that it was good. It was so slow: I could feel each stroke as he slipped into me, and I'd never been fucked slowly enough to feel that before, normally only able to feel the collision of a man's body into mine, never the calculated penetration of a cock moving into me.

And he talked during sex in new ways. He said, "You have so much life waiting to come out of you." He said, "Do you have any idea how much better you make the world?"

I had my eyes closed the whole time; it was too civilized for me to cum.

———

A few months later, Robert began growing weary of my dismal logic, my asthmatic viewpoint that no matter what we breathed, all of the world would end soon.

He said, "Life's too short."

I said, "You got that right."

He said, "You don't get it. You really don't understand. These are your only years on this planet and this is how you want to spend them?"

———

He invited me to things I didn't even know existed. "What's a silence retreat?" I asked.

"It will be great. We spend the whole weekend meditating, never speaking a word."

"Why?"

"To think."

"I've thought before, and it didn't really work out for me."

"My little stand-up comedian."

"I'm actually lying in a bath."

He sighed.

———

A few weeks later. "Would you like to hear some music tonight?" he said.

"What kind?"

"My friend Carlos's drum circle."

"I don't do drum circles, Robert."

"It will be a blast. A bunch of my friends from Burning Man will be there."

"Why don't you call me after they board the mother-ship and fly back to their planet?"

"This is getting tedious," he said.

———

"What do you enjoy about dating me?" he said, the next week. "We don't like any of the same things. We're not progressing."

"I have fun when it's just you and me," I said.

"But I need a girlfriend who's involved in all facets of my life."

"Even the drum circles?"

"I need more from you!" he said, the first time he'd ever raised his voice.

"This is all I can give!"

"Extend yourself!"

"Spare me the New Age bullshit!"

"If that's really how you feel," he said, "then this is good-bye."

"Good-bye!" I said. "Have a groovy, totally righteous life, man!" hating that we'd finally screamed at each other and it wasn't going to lead to sex.

———

And that was it. He left. I left. We left. Someone left, and I went on to the next doomed relationship, maybe the guy who shaved my head, I can't keep track of the timelines anymore. Might have been the one who put a cigarette out on my copy of *The Bell Jar*. Of all the men from my life, Robert was the only one I regretted, privately lamenting that I couldn't get over my own stigmas to date a nice guy. Why did I see kindness in a man as some sort of character flaw? Why did I put self-involved misogynists on some sort of ridiculous pedestal, giving them a bird's eye view as they treated me like a dog? I wasn't sure, but I did know that after every miserable relationship dried up and sloughed away, I always thought about Robert, asking me to be more involved in all facets of his life, because no one else had ever wanted that from me.

I remember, after that other genius I'd dated had dropped my toothbrush in the toilet, thinking about Robert. I stood at the sink, rinsing it off because I was late for work and there was no time to go buy a replacement. I remember thinking that if I had to choose between putting Robert's tepid vegan food in my mouth or a urine-drenched toothbrush, why was I choosing this?

———

Derek had used the word *wiggled*, and it was early evening when I decided to call Robert. I didn't want to call any of the girls I had happy hour with – *friends* would be too strong a word – and I couldn't bear the idea of listening to another of my mom's vague lectures.

Robert didn't answer, but this was the outgoing message on his cell: *I'll get back to you soon because, at this moment, you matter more to me than any other matter.*

"Hi, Robert. It's Mired. How are you? Can I see you? I need to see you." I started crying. "I really need to see you and I hope you call me back. I know I sound crazy right now but please call. Please. Something's happened. Something awful and I don't know what to do."

I hung up. I counted to one hundred and paced around the kitchen. I wondered where Derek was, where Robert was. I saw the plastic flower Frank had given me. Plastic flowers and fake teeth. Facades. Tricks. Veneers. I saw that appalling plastic flower sitting by the window, behind the kitchen sink. I ran my tongue over my impostors. I set my cell phone on the counter. I walked to the fake flower and yanked it from the windowsill;

it had fooled its last bee. I flipped the garbage disposal on. I stuck the flower's bud into the disposal and I let myself smile immensely because there was no one there to know how ugly my face was, and as it chewed the bud to pieces, I slowly fed the stem to the shrilling beast until it was all gone.

MIRED: THE PINEAPPLE PHENOMENON

I stood in the kitchen, staring at the empty pint glass where the flower used to be. I knocked it into the sink, but it didn't break and I lost the verve to break it. I lost the verve for everything. My dad was dead, and Derek had left me, and Robert wasn't home, and if I told my mom what had happened she'd find a way to make it my fault. Sick as it sounds, Derek was my best friend and he was the one who'd done this to me.

I locked the front door, turned off the lights in the kitchen, the hallway, the one in the bedroom. I kicked the crumpled page from our couple's journal that I'd written and ripped out, the one that said: *I have to change. You have to change. Can you do that?* I put my earplugs in deep and pulled the covers over my head and shut my eyes. It was 7:15.

––––––

It wasn't a dream, really, but while I was in bed, my ears wonderfully clogged to block out everything, I remembered Tipsy, a game Derek and I used to play. Lovely hindsight: we'd normally do it as we were getting ready to go out drinking, or sometimes we'd do it to cheer each other up. I'd stagger around in circles like I was drunk, swaying and swaying, and Derek would say, "Excuse me, is everything all right with you?" and I wouldn't answer but wobble more seriously, nearly falling, and he'd say, "Do you need me to call a doctor?" and I'd say, "I'll be okay if I get my medicine," and he'd say, "What's your medicine?" and I'd say, "They serve it at the bar down the street."

I'd keep stumbling around in small circles, never too far away from Derek because Tipsy always ended with me slowly falling over and he would swoop in and catch me, pick me up like a hero, saying, "Is there a doctor in the house? Is anyone here a trained medical professional?" Then he'd look me in the eyes and say, "There's nothing to worry about. I'll make sure you get what you want."

―――――

I pulled my earplugs out and checked my cell phone for messages. One new one. From Robert, saying he was glad to hear from me and that my message had him very worried and I should call back no matter the time. He was really worried, he said. Really. Worried. He was worried about me.

I called him back. When he answered, I said, "Hey, you."

"What happened?"

"Can I see you?"

"When?"

"Now, please."

"Where would you like to meet?" he asked.

―――――

It was too late for Robert and me to get a nice dinner, so we ended up at some crappy 24-hour diner. I met him out front. He smiled and waved as he walked up to me, but his smile vanished as he saw my face.

"Mired, what happened?"

"I don't want to talk about it until we've had a glass of wine."

"Are you okay?"

"Not at all."

He opened the door for me. The only other customer in the whole place was a fat man wearing black overalls, tools still strapped to his waist while he ate his meal and read the sports page.

Frank Sinatra sang from speakers in the ceiling, promising

some stupid woman that the best was yet to come. And the poor thing probably believed him. And worse, I probably would have, too.

Since I'd moved out of my mother's house, she'd only said one smart thing to me the whole time. We'd been talking about a bartender I was dating. He was cerebral and beautiful, but he drank too much. I was telling my mom that I thought he'd change, that he was only twenty-six and he'd get his life together because he had immense potential and could succeed at anything he wanted to.

"Potential?" she scoffed. "Potential... he won't change."

"You've never even met him."

"I don't need to meet him. What I'm saying has nothing to do with him."

"I don't understand, Mom."

"People aren't potential. We aren't who we want to be. We're only who we are right now. Either you love him for who he is, or he'll never be the right man for you."

"Was Dad the right man for you?"

"Still is," she said.

"What about Aaron?"

Aaron was her new husband. They'd been married for three years. She sent me an email a few days after their ceremony. Nothing fancy, the email was nice enough to inform me, just something simple at City Hall.

"Aaron is a close second," she said to me. "And Aaron coming in second place to your father is nothing to shake a stick at."

Sinatra was still duping that poor woman. Robert and I sat in a burgundy booth. Our menus had gleaming pictures of food next to the names of the dishes.

"I must really want to see you," Robert said. "Vegans don't normally frequent these types of establishments."

Our server came over to the table. He looked exactly like

Derek, an older version of Derek, fifty, fifty-five, the little amount of hair he had left on the sides and back of his head was shaved into a ringing crew cut. He also had a weird habit of rocking onto the balls of his feet, then setting himself down again, then rocking back onto the balls. He stood like he'd been pulled over by the highway patrol and was faking his way through field sobriety tests.

"Any drinks?" our server asked.

"What would you like?" Robert said.

"Do you have champagne?" I asked old bald Derek. His eyes were bloodshot. I stared at him, couldn't stop staring.

"We've got beer and wine only."

"Champagne is sparkling wine."

"Our wines don't sparkle."

"Are you sure?"

"I've worked here nineteen years."

"I'll take a glass of house red, then. What would you like?" I said to Robert.

"Do you have chamomile tea?"

"Nope," old bald Derek said, rocking back and forth, squinting and yawning, rocking back and forth, waiting to be read his Miranda rights and spend the night in jail.

"What kinds of tea do you have?" Robert said.

"Hot and cold," old bald Derek said. "What other kinds are there?"

"Hot sounds good," Robert said, and the waiter walked away. Then to me: "This is San Francisco, right?"

"Outside these walls, yes it is. But here at Shaky's Diner, we could be anywhere in America."

"May I ask what happened to your face and arm?"

Instinctively, I brought my good hand up and covered my mouth, felt the bottom of my fake teeth with my thumb. "I'm sorry you have to see me like this."

"Please tell me."

I brought my hands into my lap. "I think Derek broke up with me. That's my current boyfriend."

"I figured."

"I think we're through."

"Is that good or bad?" he said.

"I don't know yet."

Old bald Derek brought our drinks and said, "Is there anything else I can do for you?" I ordered without saying a word, only pointed at a picture of a club sandwich.

"Comes with fries, house salad, or fruit."

I nodded. "What kind of fruit?"

"Mostly pineapple. It's not fresh, though. It's from a can."

I shrugged. "I'm not too proud for canned fruit."

"Fruit?" Robert said to me. "I thought you were craving grease."

"I'm complicated."

"That's for sure." Robert asked him for a bowl of lemon sorbet and another glass of wine for me. Old bald Derek walked away, and Robert said, "Did Derek hurt you?"

I pulled lightly at my upper lip, massaging the skin. "Do you know I've eaten pineapple my whole life, but I have no idea how to tell if one's ripe? Sometimes I'll stand by the pineapple in the grocery store, touch a bunch of them. They all seem exactly the same. So I never buy one because what if I cut it up and it isn't ready?"

"Mired..."

"Or I cut it up and it's rotten?"

"Did he – "

"Don't you think that's weird?"

"I wouldn't know whether one's ripe or not either."

"Strange," I said. "This pineapple phenomenon."

"Did Derek hurt you?"

"It's like men. How are you supposed to pick the right ones?"

"Did he hurt you?"

"I don't know."

"How do you not know?"

"He says I fell down the stairs. Or that was what he said at first: that I fell backward down them. But now he says I wiggled out of his arms while he carried me."

"I don't understand."

I told him the circumstances of the night as best I could, then pulled my lips apart with my fingers: "These are fake teeth. My teeth are gone. I'll never see my real teeth again."

Robert maneuvered over to my side of our booth and put his arm around me. He wore new cologne that smelled like maple syrup. "You're going to be all right."

"That doesn't feel possible anymore."

"Have a sip of your wine," Robert said.

When old bald Derek brought our food, my club sandwich didn't look anything like the picture from the menu, another awful impostor. The pineapple was more beige than yellow, soft when I pushed it with my fork.

"Now that's the pineapple phenomenon," Robert said. "I wouldn't eat that. I wouldn't eat any of it."

"I was craving grease."

"Mission accomplished."

I didn't know what else to tell him. I'd been betrayed; I was furious, sad, lost; no one to blame, not even Derek; I could only impugn myself; if Derek hadn't of done it, the next drunkard would have; they didn't even matter; they were composites anyway, merges of one another; all except Robert, the only man I'd known who wanted to make me happy. Why was I trying to make Derek a better man when there was a better man sitting with me, one who didn't need to be emotionally potty-trained by Dr. Montahugh, one who didn't derive any pleasure from fighting, or lashing out, or drinking whiskey until his life froze like a fossil? The answer to my problems wasn't trying to fix Derek. I couldn't change him. Maybe Derek couldn't even do that.

"Are you dating anyone?" I asked Robert.

"No."

"Are you still attracted to me?"

"Of course."

"Even like this?"

"Absolutely."

"I need you to touch me."

Robert didn't say anything.

"I need you to put your hands on me."

"Let's talk for a while," he said.

"No more talking."

"But it seems like you need emotional support right now."

"You're right. I do. And we will talk about all this. There's so much I want to say to you. Robert, I'm realizing how many fucking mistakes I've made in my life, how ridiculously harder I've made everything. I need to stop drinking. I have to. Obviously, I'll finish this glass of wine first." I held it up toward him and he cheers'd me with his teacup. "But I'm serious. Things have to change. I've been waiting for them to do it on their own, but I don't think that's how it works. But these are things for later. That's what I'll worry about after this glass of wine. Right now, Robert, I need you to take me to your apartment and touch me."

"Are you sure this is what you want?"

"This is what I want, yes. I want to finish this wine and I want your hands on my body and then I'll get to work on the rest of it. Will you help me?"

"Of course."

"Will you help me do something I've never really done?"

"What?"

"Learn," I said. "Help me learn."

———

The terrible food eaten, the check paid, the walk to the car, the drive, the parking, the jaunt up his stairs, the key in the lock, the smell of his apartment – like chemically impersonated pine trees – and we were in the kitchen, kissing and licking and biting and sucking and my mouth hurt but I didn't care, Robert picked me up and set me on the kitchen table and pulled my shirt off, and he said, "Right here," pointing to his ear and I licked the lobe, and Robert flicked my nipple and I inhaled sharply and he dropped a hand to my pussy and rubbed it through my clothes; I raised my hips so he could slide off my skirt and panties, Robert slapped lightly on it, and I gasped, panted, and Robert pushed me back, lying on the table, his head now between my legs, I sucked in air and his spit dripped down, and his tongue, his dexterous contorting gentle tongue, its agility making me arch my back in rapture, making me pinch my nipples and push my tits together, Robert's wonderful tongue had learned some new techniques: he'd learned to lick slowly, delicately, the tip of his tongue barely grazing my clit in a luscious agony, and the initial itches of cumming spread through my body. I'd never had an orgasm with him before. I yelled, "Tell me I have a beautiful smile," and he didn't say anything and I said, "Tell me I have the most beautiful teeth you've ever seen," and he didn't say anything and I said, "Say you love my teeth," and he didn't answer so I said, "Say you love them!" really screaming now, in the midst of my orgasm, shuddering, bucking, my thighs squeezing his head, feet flexing involuntarily. Robert kept his tongue working, grunting his answer awkwardly, "Yes, I love your smile," and I said, "Do you love my teeth?" and he said, "Yes, I love your teeth," and I said, "Tell me that you love my teeth," and he said, "I love all of your teeth," and my pleasure was wholly unaffected by the fact he was lying to me.

———

After it was over, I pushed Robert away and curled up on the floor in his pine-scented kitchen and cried.

"How can I help?" he said.

"He dropped me down the stairs and ruined my face."

Robert fell to the linoleum, fell to me, hugged me. "Are you absolutely sure he did this on purpose?"

"He can't get away with it. They can't keep treating me like a dog," I said, and we stayed like that for an hour, lying on the hard bottom of the room.

FRANK: I, THE AUTEUR

Every single person on the planet made me nauseated, incited a belligerent wonder with their unmistakable obviousness and soulless stagger, and I was finally ready to watch the woman's begging face stare at the camera; I was ready to hear her whimper *please, please*, her tiny bursts of words, panhandling for clemency, her words impossible like Gordian knots and her face fixed dead center in the frame.

I probably sound like Derek. These sound like the sorts of things that he would say. But how can I not sound like him? How can I evade it? Because I think he might be right. He may have been right all along.

It felt so lambently obvious. Wasn't our collective sickness what I'd been trying to explicate with *The Unveiled Animal*? Aren't I, the auteur, who sought to investigate our despicable emotions? Wasn't I willing to examine all the ugly crevices of our natures? Doesn't that make me brave?

The answer is yes. The answers are yes. Resounding and boisterous yeses.

You see, change is always terrifying to the mainstream, always seen through a prism of chaos and panic and impotent horror, and I was willing to shatter conventions. So after Flo fired me and Mired threw me out of her apartment, I rushed home because the first thing I had to do was watch my banished masterpiece. I'd been wrong to spurn it as criminal. It wasn't a sick memento, some despondent reminder that I didn't want to turn into our old man or Derek. It was a sick memento, sure, but of something else entirely. Humankind. I'd been singling myself out, and I couldn't do that, shouldn't do that. We're all just peas in our oversized overcrowded overworked overtired polluted abused withering congested pod. We're all indistinguishable. We're all twins.

I'd wasted years as a pitiful corporate mule, loaded with pointless responsibilities. I hadn't been an unveiled animal, but completely veiled. Prostrated. Obscured from any speckles of relevance. Answer me this: why do we work away the years of our lives we could actually dedicate to our dreams – our twenties, thirties, forties, fifties, half of our sixties – only to be pardoned from debasing jobs when it's too late to do anything except hobble around on replaced hips?

There would be no more minding my manners. Your Reliable Eyewitness was finished suckling safety. It was time to evolve.

So I'd reinvent the wheel with *The Unveiled Animal*.

Yes, reinvention.

Yes, renaissance.

I made sure the door was locked. Cinching every window so no tawdry noises slipped from my privacy. Shutting windows, shades, blinds, curtains. Guaranteeing privacy, sequestering myself from any possible surveillance, any distractions or interruptions or unwanted guests. I needed to be alone with the woman who almost changed my life. The one I'd felt an immense allegiance with when I first saw her sitting in the park, holding her book. Watching her flip pages and feeling a kindred and naked alienation. Because until the moment when the man approached her and feigned criminal intent, I was falling in love with her. Each second of recorded film merely bolstered our bond: her isolation intersecting with and soldering to mine. Not a devious or lecherous love. Not the sort of amorphous obligation I typically felt toward women. Picking them up in clubs or women from the office or friends of friends. Sometimes, I wondered if I was too intellectual for sex. I could never relax. Watching their faces and bodies. Looking at my own weird limbs in mirrors during the staged prance. The whole thing seemed insipid, clumsy; we seemed insipid and clumsy.

An old lover once said to me during sex, "You look like you're studying for an exam. Relax."

"I'm relaxed."

"You look preoccupied."

"I'm not."

"Are you sure you're having fun?"

My erection was going. "I was fine."

I pressed play on my banished masterpiece and traveled time, reliving the entire experience.

Then I relived it again.

And again.

And I have to tell you, I was prepared to feel shame, regret, dismay, repugnance, but I didn't. Those things didn't even exist; they were extinct. All the guilt I'd carried about our volatile invasion into their lives was gone. And it had left because of Mired. The way she had no idea about her own life. The stupid way she categorically defended Derek. I couldn't believe it; she'd only known him for four years, four stupid years! I went out of my way to tell her the truth, and she rejected the overwhelming evidence. Perhaps, it was another part of *The Unveiled Animal*, the way we fortify ourselves from unwanted aspects of reality.

I watched the footage six more times, and right as the seventh was starting, right when the girl walked up the path, sat on the bench, and pulled out her book, my phone rang. It was Derek.

"Perfect timing," I said.

"Huh?"

"I happen to be watching what will someday be your Oscar nominated role," and saying the word *Oscar* reminded me of Flo, how people like her would never understand the nature of artists: she was too worried about making money and never wearing the same pair of shoes to the office: she was anesthe-tized into a stupor and missing out on what really mattered: the vibrancy of creation, of holding a mirror up to humankind, so the animals could see themselves.

"What are you talking about?" Derek said.

"Our robbery."

"You told me you got rid of that tape."

"I've always had it."

"Why didn't you tell me?"

"Never mind. Where are you?"

"I need to talk with you about Mired."

"I give up," I said. "You don't have to worry about me saying another word to her. I don't want to help Mired anymore."

"I did it, Frank."

I looked at the TV. I'd forgotten to pause it, and while we'd been talking, the girl's lover had stormed up the path, and Derek had snuck from the bushes, and now he was holding the two of them hostage, threatening their lives. I smiled. "You did what?"

Derek breathed hard. "I dropped her."

"It wasn't an accident?"

"No."

I looked at the TV, and the woman was hysterically trying to explain the situation to Derek, saying, "We do it for fun," while she bawled, but Derek said, "Are you having fun?" and Derek said, "Is this a good time?" and Derek said to her, "Are you enjoying yourself or what?"

"Are you going to tell Mired?" I asked him, because I couldn't believe what I was hearing from him. This didn't sound anything like my brother, his conscienceless life, his fortitude.

"This is the worst thing I've ever done," he said.

On the TV, Derek had the pistol pressed to the guy's scalp and the guy was crying and the woman looked right at the cam-era and said, "Please, please," and Derek said to her, "Give me one good reason why he shouldn't die," and the camera zoomed in on her bloodshot eyes, framing her face as she said, "I love him."

"I think I have to tell her the truth, Frank," he said to me, "but I don't know how to do it."

"Why confess?"

"Because I love her," he said over the phone, while on the TV, Derek said, "Does that sound like a good reason, Frank?" and on the TV, I answered him by saying, "Love is a good reason."

And so I said it into the phone to him: "Love is a good reason."

"I'm scared," he said.

On the TV, Derek said, "So I shouldn't kill him?" and I said, "No," and he said, "Are you sure?" and I said, "Yes," and seconds later, *The Unveiled Animal* was over and the screen went black.

"She'll forgive you," I said, but that wasn't what I meant. Not at all. What I meant by telling Derek that Mired would forgive him was that my movie wasn't over. The screen might have been black, but it was only intermission; it could come back to life, could wake from its protracted hibernation and change the world with the greatest moment of none-scripted cinema in history as I laugh in Flo's face and reinvent the wheel: Derek confessing his crime to Mired, his first and only confession. Derek dismissing every instinct of self-preservation that had defended him his whole life. Derek doing something vitally new to his animal, a fresh evolution.

Besides, why shouldn't I film it? I couldn't help their situation. Derek was going to continue being Derek. Mired would be Mired. Nature never surprised you. Mired had her fake facts and justifications and she had her fake teeth, and she might as well get back Derek, her phony love.

What would the world be without our slaking delusions?

Derek breathed hard again, made a choking noise into the phone.

"Are you crying?" I said.

Breathing hard again. "I'm scared."

"Of what?"

"Scared she'll end this."

I could already imagine the brilliant tableau. Derek and Mired sitting in their kitchen or living room. I'd be crouched on the bare hill behind their apartment building, dressed all in black to evade detection, filming them through the window. I'd call it *Infected Confession*. Or *Infection Confession*. The latter had a better rhythm. I'd try and have the film edited before Sundance's application deadline.

"You have to try and make things right," I said, wondering whether the European film festivals accepted submissions via the web, or if I'd have to mail them hard copies. If time was tight, this could be a problem. I said, "You have to tell her the truth, or there's no way you two can go on together."

"I know."

"Where are you?"

"Driving home."

"From where?"

"I went to Reno."

"Why?"

"How am I supposed to do it?" he said. "How can I tell her I hurt her on purpose?"

I realized I couldn't film them from the hillside behind their apartment. The camera's microphone would never pick up the dialogue, and the dialogue was going to be what granted the scene its heart-wrenching power. I'd have to crouch in the walkway outside a window.

"How far from home are you?" I said.

"A couple hours."

"Does she know you're coming?"

"No."

"Are you going to give her a heads up?"

"Should I?"

It sounded too risky for my movie. I needed to capture the shock on her face as she heard his key in the lock. I wanted to film their faces staring at each other for the first time since Derek had disappeared. "I wouldn't," I said. "It's better to talk about these things face to face."

I imagined Derek scouring his paltry vocabulary to try and clear his name. Imagined Mired, aghast, shaking her head, but in the end forgiving him, because, really, who else would want to put up with either of them? They were better off stalking the same sordid habitat.

"I guess you're right," Derek said. Then my twin brother said something I hadn't heard him say in years, and the times I had heard him say it, I knew he wasn't telling the truth: "Thank you. Really, Frank. Thanks."

"You don't have to thank me."

"I know you don't approve, but thanks for being there for me."

"I'll be there," I said. "No doubt I'll be there," I said and wished him luck. Then I hung up, grabbed my video camera, and ran out the door to capture the climax of their bizarre, sadistic tale.

PART 3
WHAT WENT RIGHT?

THE UNVEILED ANIMALS

It was lousy feeling all that doom. Lousy when I finally pulled up in front of our apartment, no easy feat without the GPS. Lousy seeing those stairs, walking up those stairs, lousy wanting to run away again. I'd have even fled to my mom's house, but she probably wouldn't tolerate me, her intolerable kin. Did she wonder whether any good would grow in her no-good son?

I made it to the top of the stairs. Lights off in our apartment. I put the key in quietly and snuck inside. Crept down the hallway, hunting for Mired. Our bedroom door was open, but she wasn't in bed. I walked toward the bathroom and kicked something on the floor. A piece of wadded paper that I leaned down and picked up and read: *I have to change. You have to change. Can you do that?* She must have ripped it from our journal, that book of shame, must have ripped it for using the word *you* so many times, a no-no. But how could she avoid saying *you*? How was she supposed to blame anyone but me?

I shoved the piece of paper in my pocket, walked to the bathroom, the living room. She wasn't in either. I went into the kitchen and sat down.

―――――

I showered at Robert's house, then he drove me home. He said, "Why won't you stay with me tonight?" and I said, "I'd rather be by myself." But as we pulled into my building's parking lot, I saw Derek's truck sitting there. The latest to be immortalized on my Mt. Rushmore of Male Failures had snuck back, enshrined in ugly memory for the rest of my life. The lights in our apartment were on.

"What are you going to do?" Robert said.

————

I'd gone around the back of their building. Up the back stairs. I was down the walkway from the laundry room. I was four or five feet from their kitchen window, huddled in the shadows. Waiting. It was chilly.

Their kitchen light finally went on. My brother barged in, sat down, then immediately got back up and retrieved a shot glass from the cabinet and poured himself some whiskey. I smiled, thrilled that he went for alcohol, his Achilles' heel, the kindling to spark my movie. He sat down at the table again, finished his glass in a sip and poured some more. I put the camera to my eye, pressed record, marking the beginning of *Infection Confession*. Some footage of Derek drinking in anticipation of Mired coming home might really give the film a sense of looming bedlam, the serenity before the squall.

This was going to be the first time my brother had ever done the right thing, and I'd capture every second, every frame revealing another contortion of our flimsy spirit.

————

The termites went to work again. They must have had a union, a strong union, the teamsters of the parasite kingdom. They'd enjoyed a good stint without having to punch the clock and rip me up, but here they were again, gnawing and gnawing.

I didn't want to see her mangled face again, couldn't imagine seeing what I'd done, and I shouldn't have had any more whiskey.

————

Robert said, "Do you want me to go up there with you?" and I said, "I'll be all right," and he said, "Mired, he already hurt you once," and I said, "I'm aware of that," and he said, "Can I walk you to the door?" and I said, "I'll be all right," and he said, "I'm walking you to the door," and I said, "Fine."

He was the only man I'd ever known who actually wanted to make me feel good and now even wanted to hold my hand as I interrogated Derek about his betrayal.

"I'm glad you're with me," I said to Robert. He was a good man, maybe too good: I couldn't imagine myself with an optimistic vegan Buddhist, couldn't imagine what I could offer him except grief.

"I really missed you," he said.

———

Derek slamming his fist on the kitchen table. Derek pushing the bottle of whiskey away from him. Knocking the shot glass over and it rolled off of the table and onto the floor. Not leaning down to get it. Me zooming in all the way to capture the slightest gestures of his pathos.

———

I promised myself no more whiskey, but the bottle still sat on the table. My glass was only on the floor. I could get them, use them. I couldn't see a single scratch on her face without the termites pulling on executioners' masks and finishing me off, without their fangs being dipped in poison and every bite bringing my lousy life to its end.

I leaned over and picked up my glass, set it on the table, and I kept thinking about the whiskey's power to protect me from seeing Mired's face. I'd look at her but with enough whiskey in me, her scabs and stitches wouldn't look like allegations.

———

Robert and I stood at the bottom of the stairs. He tried to take my hand, the broken one. I flinched. "I'm not going to hurt you," he said, gracefully wrapping his hand around my cast. He said, "We don't have to go up there. Come home with me."

"I need to know," I said, and he said, "You already know."

"I need to hear him say it," I said, and he said, "How will that help?"

"I never said it would help," I said, "just that I need to hear it."

"This isn't a good idea."

But I needed to see him, needed to hear it right from his mouth, the way victims' families sometimes wanted to watch the guilty get electrocuted or hanged or lethally injected – agonizing but vital healing.

———

A door slamming down the back walkway. Heavy footsteps walking. Coming my way. I dropped the camera from my eye, curled up in a little ball on the floor. Hoping the darkness and my black clothes would conceal me. The door to the laundry room opening, closing. Thirty seconds later an old dryer wheezed itself to life. The laundry door opened again, the footsteps walking away from me. Me leaping up and pointing the camera back at my brother and wondered what he was thinking and feeling, wondering if he knew I was out here. This would be his greatest vanquishing yet, defeating his own instinct at self-preservation. Maybe that should be the film's title: *Beating Myself and Winning the World*.

———

No more. I took the whiskey bottle to the sink, ready to pour it out. If I dumped it, I couldn't drink anymore, and I needed to stop drinking. I took the cap off, held the bottle over the sink. All I had to do was turn it upside down, that was all, but I couldn't bring myself to pour it out so I screwed the cap back on. I didn't want to see her mangled face stare at me, demanding an explanation. I'd need every shield I could find so I didn't knock out my own teeth then say to her, "See? Do you see how sorry I am? Do you see I'm the sorriest I've ever been in my whole lousy fucking life?"

———

Robert and I were at the top of the stairs. I looked back at them. It was weird to see something I'd walked on, that I'd occupied casually so many different times over the years. They were reminders, planks of disappointment showing that I hadn't made any progress, like one of those machines at the gym, where people walked up a belt of revolving stairs, making no headway: those malicious machines where you never went anywhere.

———

My brother stood with the whiskey at the sink. The bottle shook in his shaking hand. He was crying.

———

Under the kitchen sink was a toolbox. In the toolbox was a hammer. And if I couldn't pour the whiskey out myself maybe the hammer could help. The hammer could get rid of the whiskey without a second thought. It wasn't worried about seeing her. The hammer didn't have a care in the world and I'd felt that way for a long time but not anymore. I took it out of the toolbox and lay the bottle in the sink and held the hammer above it.

———

Robert said, "Are you sure you're ready to see him?" and I said, "I don't know," and he said, "We can turn around and leave right now," and I said, "I need to know," and he said, "Can I please come in there with you? I'm worried."

Then we heard the sound of smashing glass coming from inside the apartment.

———

My brother setting the bottle in the sink. My brother hovering the hammer above the bottle. My brother hammering down on it and crying harder. Me taking a step toward him, then stepping back, remembering I needed to keep my distance, but wanting to walk all the way to the window, to capture this scene in as much detail as I possibly could. I'd never seen Derek so upset and I liked it. There was a desperation present that he never exposed, shrouded in his reckless behavior, but he'd done something that he couldn't evade, ignore, and I wondered why now, why after all these years of brazenness was he finally deciding to do the right thing? That would be one of the whispered motifs of my film – the way a neglected, hoarse conscience can get its voice back and sing.

———

And the hammer crashed down on the bottle and whiskey splashed all over me and tiny insects of glass ricocheted everywhere, and then I walked over and picked up the shot glass and set it in the middle of the kitchen table and smashed it, too, kept smashing the bits into smaller bits and then into smaller ones, finally into some kind of shining dust. I set the hammer on the table and I sat at the table and I rested my head on the table, on top of the smashed glass and shining dust, and it dug into my forehead, and that was when it happened: the glass in my forehead gagging the termites, every tooth of theirs suddenly still, engines off. The harder I pressed my head against the glass it was like I'd never housed a termite in my entire life, and maybe this was a way to throw these cannibals out of me. I stood up and took every bit of broken glass, the shining dust, the pieces of the whiskey bottle from the sink and threw them all on the floor, then took off my shoes and socks and tap-danced all around the room as shards of glass lodged in my feet, freeing me.

———

The front door wasn't locked. I took a step inside and said, "Derek?"

———

Mired shouting my brother's name. Mired moving into the kitchen. Some stray guy following behind her and holding her casted hand awkwardly. Derek stopping his weird dance, the dance that made his face wince as his bare feet shimmied on the broken glass.

He looked at Mired. Derek noting the man. Derek asking, "Who's that?"

164

I looked up and saw Mired and her mangled face, and there was no whiskey left to protect me, and I'd stopped dancing so the termites started spooning me up with huge melon-ballers again. Mired didn't answer when I asked who the guy was.

She said, "What are you breaking?" and I said, "The glass is helping," and she said, "Why do you have a hammer?"

———

He didn't look like himself: crying, barefoot, bloodied footprints all over the floor. He didn't look like Frank either. This was someone else, someone new, he and Frank's lost triplet. The one who couldn't keep the toxic truth locked up. The one who wanted to tell me the truth, I could tell. This one was honest and I'd finally know.

"Tell me how I wiggled out of your arms," I said.

He slapped his hands on his thighs and said, "You just wiggled," and I said, "Liar."

———

I took two steps toward their kitchen window. The guy putting his hands up in acquiescence after Derek asked who he was and Mired pointing at the hammer and saying what was it for and calling Derek a liar and me smiling and trying not to laugh, trying to contain myself, and you're probably smiling, too. Admit it. We're both here for the same reason: to see what happens next.

———

There are tiny differences between my face and Frank's face, and as I stared at Mired, with her bruises and the swelling in her cheeks and scabbed forehead, she looked like her own twin, a haggard clone, young Darla.

"Frank told me what you did," she said.

———

I wanted to hear the lost triplet say it. I wanted him to look me in the eyes and use the word *wiggle*. I didn't think he'd be able to do it, and if somehow he conjured the crucial audacity, I'd know the truth anyway. The truth had smashed glass and bloodied the soles of his feet. The truth had used a hammer.

———

A door slamming. A door slamming and footsteps dull thudding down the walkway. Me taking two steps back, into the shadows. I should have been collapsing to the ground and cowering again, but I wasn't willing to stop filming. I wasn't going to miss this topnotch proof about our animal's disfigured intentions; I wasn't going to come so close, only to skulk home empty-handed to wonder if my life would be better if I ever had the nerve to follow through with something. I was going to follow through right now.

Footsteps still dull thudding down the walkway. Getting closer.

———

"What did Frank tell you?" I said to her, mashing my feet harder on the glass, which helped with the termites but maybe telling her the truth would be some kind of termite apocalypse. Maybe saying it out loud, saying to her – Mired, I lost my temper and overreacted and I'm sorry and I love you and I hope you can find it in your heart to forgive me and I really mean it this time: I want to be a better man.

"He told me you did it on purpose, and I need to hear you say it," she said.

"Me, too."

"You too what?"

"Me, too," I said.

———

Any second the words I had to hear would ooze out of him, more pollution from his sinister gender. All the men and all their lies. Their briberies. They preserved their patriarchal right to degrade women like it was an undescended testicle of the US Constitution.

The lost triplet gazed at me. We stood by the kitchen table. The lost triplet shook his head in frustration, working up the courage to tell me what Derek had done. The hammer sat on the kitchen table.

"Let's all calm down," Robert said.

"Robert, I have to do this. I need to hear it. If you want to leave, I understand." Then I looked at Derek: "Is it that hard for you to be honest with me?"

"I'm trying to be better than Daryl," he said.

"Who's Daryl?"

"I'm going to try."

I picked up the hammer.

———

Dull thudding footsteps rounding the corner and walking toward the laundry room. Me standing, holding the camera toward Derek and Mired. Me refusing to hide. The person maybe forty feet away. Whistling "The Star Spangled Banner." A little overweight with short hair. It was probably a woman. I couldn't tell. Derek and Mired really yelling at each other now. My camera gobbled up every perfect second of footage. My camera the first to feast on the bounty of the moment. This was all I'd ever wanted. This was every prayer being answered. Every time I begged Jesus, Buddha, Mohammed, Zeus, Brahma, whoever was eavesdropping on our dilapidated zoo, for the opportunity to make something of my life. It was here. It was finally happening. Filmmaking would never be the same. It had a new sovereign genre dedicated to telling people the truth about our animal. Reinventing the wheel. Instead of words and behavior being chosen for the actors, now the actors truly revealed the splendor and woe of our hearts without any artificial conceits: we had the truth and what else did we need?

———

Mired and her lousy bodyguard were only a few feet away from me, but all they stood on was naked linoleum and I was

167

on the broken glass. I was drunk. I was a drunk. I was our dad. I was mean. I was a liar. I was a terrible person. I wasn't loved enough. I wasn't loving enough. I wasn't patient enough. I was lousy. I was dead with rot and guilt. The termites were finishing the job.

"Say it," Mired said.

———

The man in front of me oscillated between Derek and the lost triplet. Derek trying to lie, the triplet trying to sneak out the truth, a war going on inside their body, a shimmering malfunction.

———

Inching toward Derek and Mired despite the dull thuds and whistle walking toward the laundry room. I couldn't put the camera down, too close to capturing the moment of Derek at his most vulnerable, frail, meager, at the moment of his wicked confession.

This time next year I'd be a household name and Flo would watch me on the Oscars. I'd be famous not because of good looks or nepotism but because of artistic merit, my purity and integrity. *Infection Confession*, working title for the first *Unveiled Animal* film, would be perfectly received because every human loved to learn the secrets of others, so greedy with our unashamed invasions of privacy.

———

She held up the hammer, termites floating out of my body in lifeboats through the cuts in my feet, leaving my village before the soldiers opened fire. I didn't know what to tell her, how to tell her. There was no way for me to make her understand. No way to defend myself. No desire to defend myself. A perfect score on the lousy-scale. Another relentless fiasco. Our broken-down world with its liars and bastards and rage and why couldn't we stop hurting one another? Why couldn't there be a day naked of our corrosions? The sad way we sputter around this fragile galaxy molesting life.

I don't need to remind you of all of them. All their dishonesty. Shaving my head or punching my picture of Frida Kahlo or pissing on my shoes or putting a cigarette out on *The Bell Jar* or all of the other violations.

I held the hammer up right in his face. "Tell me why."

———

The dull thuds stopping. Whistling stopping. There wasn't the sound of the laundry room door opening. Only a voice saying to me, "What do you think you're doing?" but I couldn't take the camera away from the kitchen. The dull thuds picking back up and thudding past the laundry room, toward me. The voice, either high for a man or low for a woman, saying, "Hey, I'm talking to you. I'm calling the cops if you don't answer." The voice saying, "I'm calling 911," then dull thudding in the opposite direction.

———

I said, "Go ahead," and Mired said, "I'll do it," and the guy said, "Don't hit him," and I said, "Fucking hit me!" and the guy grabbed her shoulder and said, "Don't do this," but she said, "Get your fucking hands off of me!" and she kept shaking the hammer so the guy let his hand fall away from her and took a few steps back and rubbed his face, and I said, "Come on, do it," and put my arms out like I was Jesus nailed to the cross and flexed my hands and I smiled right at her, did my best to wink right at her like our old man, saying, "Please," and I meant it, really I meant it, because her hitting me with the hammer might be the medicine to banish the remaining termites, a total eradication, genocide. A way to forget my My Lai. Maybe the hammer could absolve me from the crime, or maybe salvation was further away than that.

———

I said, "Please tell me."

I said, "I have a right to know."

I said, "I have a right to know and you have a responsibility to tell me the truth." Derek and the lost triplet had stared me in the eyes this whole time, but now their gaze fell to the linoleum, their arms still outstretched, mouth still smiling. They nodded slowly, yes, yes. They kept nodding. They nodded and nodded, yes, yes, and I said, "You hurt me on purpose?" and they nodded twice more and stopped.

My mom was right: people weren't who they wanted to be: we only exist as we are now, right this second: we hold hammers in people's faces or outstretch our arms like Christ writhing in anguish: we aren't the person we want to be: we are defined by the last words out of our mouths and our last actions executed.

Derek was still smiling right in my face, all those teeth teasing me like little white tyrants. And I hit him in the mouth with the hammer.

———

Derek collapsing in a heap after the hammer's impact. I couldn't see him anymore, could only see Mired standing there with the bloody hammer, staring at it, wailing now, dropping it on the floor. I knew I shouldn't walk all the way to their window, but I couldn't stop myself. I needed the ending, the actors not acting but reacting, stunned by one another, perfectly human, perfect evolutions. And I walked right up to the window. Derek lay there, covering his vandalized mouth, blood pouring seeping teeming down his hands, his arms, soaking his shirt. Derek screaming. Derek kicking his legs.

Mired sitting down at the kitchen table. Mired sobbing. Mired lost.

The guy saying to her, "Does Derek have a twin?" and pointing at the window, at me. I ducked. Him saying, "He's right there with a video camera," and shaking Mired and her not answering and shaking again and finally her snapping out of it and saying, "Frank?"

Your Reliable Eyewitness, still crouched, inching away from them along the building's wall.

Mired saying, "Is that you, Frank?"

Her saying, "Are you filming this?"

Me slipping my camera in my backpack.

Mired saying, "Frank, is that really you?" and me galloping down the walkway on my hands and knees, and Mired called after me, "Frank! Stop!"

Me looking back and her head sticking out the window and us seeing each other and Mired calling, "Stop, Frank!"

Me not stopping. Me galloping on. No reason to stop myself, with the movie in my camera and the camera in my backpack. Me finding no words to send back to Mired. No need to clarify why I was here. We were all after the same thing: Derek needed his confession and Mired needed his confession and I needed it, too. All of us had gorged and were happy and surfeited now that we'd gotten it.

"Frank! Stop! Please!"

Me realizing that since Mired had already seen me, there was no reason to be on hands and knees, galloping away, *evolve!*, so I grew from four-legged beast to upright man. Springing to my feet. Running down the hall.

"Frank, don't!"

Running down the stairs.

Running down Mired's stairs.

Running down them and getting in my car and driving off. Me making it away with my movie and into my apartment and shunning the protocol of cinching windows and locking doors and minding the volume. Me simply hooking the camera up to the TV and rewinding and pressing play. There was a pornography to it. Me salivating. Me stiff with anticipation. Adrenaline. Me marveling at the beauty of prayers being answered: every animal sated on the gluttony of spying.

Evolve!

The scene beginning: Derek coming into the kitchen and drinking whiskey and it wouldn't be long now until Mired was there and the guy was there and it wouldn't be long until she held the hammer in his face and the moment of his marvelous confession. All of us transfixed on his avalanche of obscene honesty. Words wobbling out of him like a faun learning to walk. Staggering with imprecision and gracelessness. It wouldn't be long now until my new life started.

PART 4
WHAT WENT RIGHT...

NEW TRICKS

Six days later, we were going back, had to go back; there was no way to avoid it.

Derek and I traveled to the dentist's office to get his mouth fit with a temporary bridge. We walked out of our kitchen, which was still demolished: broken glass, dried whiskey, his bloodied footprints all over the place. Neither of us had the energy to clean up the mess. Every morning I promised myself I'd get to it, but I never did. I knew eventually I'd have no choice but to scrub it all away.

Out of our apartment complex and down the stairs. Derek limped severely.

"I don't mind driving," I said.

"Nah."

"Let's take a taxi."

"I don't want to. Fair is fair," he said. Derek didn't say it in a mean way at all; he sounded sincere.

"This isn't about what's fair."

"Sure it is. BART's fine."

So we walked slowly. It was overcast, foggy, windy; it was San Francisco. Derek's feet must have been killing him. A construction worker slammed his jackhammer's metal beak into the asphalt, gouging deep. I motioned at the worker and he turned it off. He wore a T-shirt that said *I'm Mexican, not Latino.*

"How much longer are you going to do that?" I said to him.

"For today?"

"Until you're totally finished."

"I can't say."

"Days? Weeks? Months?" I asked.

He shrugged his shoulders, turned the urban woodpecker on, drove its beak back into the road.

I walked and Derek limped and we didn't say anything else until we rode the escalator underground, down into the BART station.

"Does it hurt?" Derek said with quite a lisp of his own now, pointing at his mouth.

"He gives you a Novocain shot, but you're still uncomfortable while he's drilling."

Derek had lost five teeth to the hammer. His bottom lip was split, a huge round scab on it that looked like a rosebud.

"Do you have any more aspirin?" he said.

I shook my head. "We were going to buy more this morning but we overslept."

"Maybe I can ask someone in the station if they have any."

"We'll be at the dentist's in fifteen minutes."

"I can't wait that long."

"The aspirin won't kick in right away. The shot numbs you immediately."

"Numb sounds good."

"Any word from Frank?" I said.

"He hasn't returned my calls."

"Mine either."

"He might not," Derek said. "We may not hear anything from him. Who knows with my family."

"I still can't believe he did it."

"I can." Derek took a deep breath, patted his hand at his mouth and winced. "In a weird way, I'm glad he finally did."

"Glad?"

"In a weird way, yeah."

"What kind of person does that make him, treating us like that?" I said.

"There's only one kind of person."

"What do you mean?"

"We're all the same."

"But he filmed us."

"Remember what we did?" He winced again. "Frank's right: we're animals."

Derek was wrong and so was his deranged brother, who I was nothing like. We weren't all the same, weren't animals. We were humans and we could learn. We could figure things out, if you gave us enough time.

Then Derek's expression changed, focused. I turned to see what he was watching: two BART cops walked toward us, one carrying a bunch of duffel bags; all of them were black, except for a bright pink one. The other cop guided a leashed German Shepherd.

They walked past us, all the way to the end of the platform. The one with the dog stayed at the far side. The other cop scattered the black duffel bags all around the platform, which was about two hundred feet long.

"What are they doing?" I said.

"I don't know."

"It's a little early in the morning for attack dogs."

"9/11 stuff, I guess," Derek said.

"That was six years ago. This must be because of Iraq and Afghanistan. Or North Korea. Or Iran. Syria. Yemen. Russia. Don't forget about China. George W. Bush is trying to end the world before history has a chance to remember him."

Derek laughed, cringed, put a hand up to his mouth. "Don't make me laugh. It hurts too much."

"Sorry."

"So am I."

We'd been apologizing to each other a lot in the days since I'd hit him. We made vague excuses to explain our soiled actions, our failures, never talking directly about what we'd done to each other, not yet anyway. The only topic we'd specifically discussed was canceling our next appointment with Dr. Montahugh. Initially, neither of us wanted her to see our faces or our fake teeth, but yesterday, Derek said that he didn't care if she saw him this way: "What difference does it really make?" he asked.

"She'll want to know what happened."

Derek stared at me in a way I hadn't seen before: "I know she will." He reached over and rubbed my cast. "I know she will and I don't care."

Now the cop had carried the pink duffel bag back down the platform with him; he set it on a bench, right next to Derek. Then he stood a few feet away from it, from us. He radioed to his partner, said, "Commence the exercise," and his partner led the dog toward the first bag.

"What's going on?" Derek said to the cop.

"Watch," he said, pointing at his partner, the dog.

The German Shepherd reached the first duffel bag, sniffed it a few times, and walked away.

"So far, so good," the cop said to us.

"What's he looking for?" Derek said.

"She."

"Huh?"

"The dog is female."

"What's she looking for?"

The cop flicked his eyebrows. "The bad guys."

"It's convenient that they fit in those little bags," I said, smirking at Derek, who was trying to keep from laughing. He frowned at me.

The cop snickered. "No, no. Not the bad guys themselves. They're not in the bags. She's learning to sniff out their hazards."

"Like bombs?" I said.

"We prefer the word *hazards*."

The dog approached the next duffel bag. Same thing: a few

seconds with her nose pressed up to it, before walking on to the next.

The cop said, "This is her last chance."

"At what?" Derek said.

"She's failed this test more times than I can count. Once more and she's out of a job." He snickered again.

"What happens to her then?" I said.

"That's a good question. I'm not sure," the cop said.

The dog walked up to the next duffel bag, sniffed its contents, and moved on.

"Let's hope it isn't true what they say," the cop said to us.

"What?" Derek said. "What?" I said. We sung it at the same time: "What?"

"About an old dog and new tricks."

"How many times has she actually failed?" I said.

"You don't want to know," the cop said, shaking his head. "She's failed so many times it's embarrassing."

"Can't she see that this one is different?" Derek said, pointing at the pink bag.

"Nope. Dogs are sort of colorblind," the cop said. "They all look the same to her."

The train that was supposed to take Derek and me downtown pulled into the station. People got off. People got on. We were supposed to get on.

Derek stood up and said to the cop, "I'll keep my fingers crossed for her."

More snickering.

I didn't get up off the bench. I couldn't leave yet. Because no matter what's happened we should all get the chance to try again. To live smarter based on what we've learned, if we've learned. The terrifying part is what if we haven't? Where do we start, how do we start, what's the first step?

"Come on," Derek said.

"You go," I said.

"What?"

"I'm going to stay and see if she gets it."

"But I'll be late for my appointment," Derek said, walking toward the train.

The dog sniffed the last black duffel bag, didn't smell anything. The other cop led her toward the pink one, toward me.

"Go ahead," I said.

"Come with me."

"I'll meet you there."

Derek stood in the train's doorway: "It's leaving. Come on."

"I have to see if she can do it."

Derek stepped inside the train. The doors closed. He stared at me. His palms on the glass. He looked like an abandoned child.

The train crept away.

I watched the dog as she got closer.

"I've got 20 dollars that says she can't sniff it out," the cop said to me.

I looked at him. The train was gone; Derek was gone. The dog was only a few steps away from the last bag, her last chance. Soon I'd see if all those mistakes were finally ready to pay off. I extended my hand toward the cop so we could shake on it, make the bet official. "I like my odds," I said to him, waiting to see what came next.

ACKNOWLEDGMENTS–INFERIORITY COMPLEX

Sometimes, when I buy a book, I read the author's Acknowledgments page first. I'm not sure why I do this because usually these kinds of pages make me feel bad about myself. I examine these sprawling litanies of gratitude and ironic inside jokes and I wonder: why is my world so small that I only have like eleven people to thank? What is that saying about me? Shouldn't I try to seem more important?

And it isn't only the length of these authors' Acknowledgements sections: it's who they're thanking. People actually hang out with Salman Rushdie? Wait a sec: someone has had the pleasure of talking shop with Amy Hempel or snorkeling with Lynda Barry? Acknowledgments pages are a name-dropping royale! It's masturbation and nepotism at their most visible, and all I've been able to deduce is that I got gypped on the whole nepotism thingy (masturbation, not so much). I mean, I'm just another sucker living in squalor. Sure, I've got my family and friends to thank, but who the hell are they?

So to mitigate my Acknowledgments-Inferiority Complex (AIC), I've decided to thank a glorious mash-up of people for their love and guidance over the years, only some of which I've ever met and yes, some are dead, while others might be fictitious. You decide which ones are real and which stink of phoniness. But I hope you suspend your disbelief; I hope you read this page and think to yourself: wow, I'm palpably impressed by Mohr's varied and distinguished menagerie of colleagues; this is an urbane ensemble indeed!

Here goes: I never would have learned to ride a bike if it wasn't for Boris Yeltsin. Kofi Annan and Quentin Tarantino have been like sisters to me. Who can forget that the Rev. Jesse Jackson bought me my first pencil and said, "Write, young man, write." I've been blessed to have a family of strong women: Jessica, Katy, Diane, Sarah, Kathryn, and Shana: if there's any empathy in this novel it's because of all you. My mentors, Jacques Cousteau and Sally Ride, who taught me to dive first and ask questions later. Bucky Sinister answered some important questions for me this year. Sasquatch gave me the belief in myself to power on despite all the skepticism thrumming in the world. Leota Antoinette is the brains behind this operation (and the heart). Britney Spears braids my cornrows. Donald Ray Pollock is the most generous writer I know. My editors at Two Dollar Radio: Roy Orbison, Freddy Krueger, Eric and Eliza Obenauf, Josh Hartnett, James Earl Jones. Robyn Russell continues to be a thoughtful reader for me, as does CY, Jen L, Kyle R, the Professor (not the one from "Gilligan's Island"; the real one), Andrew B, Robespierre, Michael L, Calder L, Jason B, Rebecca S, Liza C, and Flavor Flav. Jane Underwood of the Writing Salon is nice enough to sign my paychecks. Saddam Hussein taught me to make Belgian waffles. The beautiful cover of this book was created by Aubrey Rhodes; she's a genius, and you should buy her work. And you're probably not supposed to acknowledge one of the characters from the book itself because they're not real people and that might mean I'm schizophrenic. But I don't care: I learned more from penning Mired than I have any other character, and some day, I hope to have her strength, will, and guts to be a better person in my real life, not just in those I imagine.

Also published by **TWO DOLLAR RADIO**

SOME THINGS THAT MEANT THE WORLD TO ME
A NOVEL BY JOSHUA MOHR
A Trade Paperback Original; 978-0-9820151-1-7; $15.50 US
* *Oprah Magazine* Top 10 Terrific Read of 2009.
* *The Nervous Breakdown* Best Book of 2009.
* *San Francisco Chronicle* Bestseller.

"Mohr's first novel is biting and heartbreaking... it's as touching as it is shocking." —*Publishers Weekly* (Starred)

THE DROP EDGE OF YONDER
A NOVEL BY RUDOLPH WURLITZER
A Trade Paperback Original; 978-0-9763895-5-2; $15.00 US
* *Time Out New York*'s Best Book of 2008.
* *ForeWord* Magazine 2008 Gold Medal in Literary Fiction.
"A picaresque American *Book of the Dead*... in the tradition of Thomas Pynchon, Joseph Heller, Kurt Vonnegut, and Terry Southern." —*Los Angeles Times*

NOG
A NOVEL BY RUDOLPH WURLITZER
A Trade Paperback Original; 978-0-9820151-2-4; $15.50 US

"[*Nog*'s] combo of Samuel Beckett syntax and hippie-era freakiness mapped out new literary territory for generations to come."
—*Time Out New York*

I SMILE BACK
A NOVEL BY AMY KOPPELMAN
A Trade Paperback Original; 978-0-9763895-9-0; $15.00 US

"Powerful. Koppelman's instincts help her navigate these choppy waters with inventiveness and integrity."
—*Los Angeles Times*

Also published by **TWO DOLLAR RADIO**

THE CAVE MAN
A NOVEL BY XIAODA XIAO
A Trade Paperback Original; 978-0-9820151-3-1; $15.50 US
* WOSU (an NPR member station) Favorite Book
  of 2009.

"As a parable of modern China, [*The Cave Man*] is chilling." —*Boston Globe*

EROTOMANIA: A ROMANCE
A NOVEL BY FRANCIS LEVY
A Trade Paperback Original; 978-0-9763895-7-6; $14.00 US
* *Queerty* Top 10 Book of 2008.
* *Inland Empire Weekly* Standout Book of 2008.

"Miller, Lawrence, and Genet stop by like proud ancestors." —*Village Voice*

THE PEOPLE WHO WATCHED
HER PASS BY
A NOVEL BY SCOTT BRADFIELD
A Trade Paperback Original; 978-0-9820151-5-5; $14.50 US

"A wake-up call shouting Bradfield's humorously erudite take on modern American life." —WOSU (an NPR member station)

THE SHANGHAI GESTURE
A NOVEL BY GARY INDIANA
A Trade Paperback Original; 978-0-9820151-0-0; $15.50 US

"An uproarious, confounding, turbocharged fantasia that manages, alongside all its imaginative bravura, to hold up to our globalized epoch the fun-house mirror it deserves." —*Bookforum*